All of a sudden he heard a *thunk*. Immediately there followed the report of a gun that sounded like a rifle. Longarm felt his horse stumble, and he knew the horse had been hit and was going down. He began, moving swiftly, to get ready for his dismount. As rapidly as he could, he unwound the lead rope from the saddle horn so the pack animal would be free. In the same motion, he drew his carbine out of the boot on the right side of his saddle. His eyes were already searching the ground ahead for cover as he felt his horse go to its knees. He heard the buzz of a bullet near his ear. With his carbine in his right hand, he was just able to grab his canteen by its strap and step onto the ground as his horse, with a gurgle and a sigh, fell forward onto the sandy prairie. . . .

DON'T MISS THESE
ALL-ACTION WESTERN SERIES
FROM THE BERKLEY PUBLISHING GROUP

THE GUNSMITH by J. R. Roberts
Clint Adams was a legend among lawmen, outlaws, and ladies. They called him . . . the Gunsmith.

LONGARM by Tabor Evans
The popular long-running series about U.S. Deputy Marshal Long—his life, his loves, his fight for justice.

SLOCUM by Jake Logan
Today's longest-running action Western. John Slocum rides a deadly trail of hot blood and cold steel.

McMASTERS by Lee Morgan
The blazing new series from the creators of *Longarm*. When McMasters shoots, he shoots to kill. To his enemies, he is the most dangerous man they have ever known.

TABOR EVANS

LONGARM

AND THE ARIZONA AMBUSH

JOVE BOOKS, NEW YORK

LONGARM AND THE ARIZONA AMBUSH

A Jove Book / published by arrangement with
the author

PRINTING HISTORY
Jove edition / December 1995

ISBN: 0-515-11766-8

A JOVE BOOK®
Jove Books are published by The Berkley Publishing Group,
200 Madison Avenue, New York, New York 10016.
JOVE and the "J" design are trademarks
belonging to Jove Publications, Inc.

PRINTED IN THE UNITED STATES OF AMERICA

10 9 8 7 6 5 4 3 2 1

Chapter 1

He had been able to see the little cabin for some distance as he'd ridden slowly across the harsh, flat prairie of southeastern Arizona. Sometimes there would be a low place and he'd only be able to see the top half of the cabin, but then he'd strike a rise and be able to see the whole structure. It stuck out like a sore thumb in the vastness of the high plains which didn't seem fit to nurture even varmints, much less human beings and their animals. It was the only thing in sight much taller than a man. Off in the distance, looking deceptively close, were buttes and single mountains that would rise to heights of five and six thousand feet, but the cabin was the only thing that bespoke the presence of man in any direction for miles and miles.

He was coming straight at the cabin, directly from the front. To his eye, it looked deserted. He had no intention, however, of making straight for the place without giving it a lengthy and thorough inspection. The man he was trailing was the worst kind; he was mean and he was smart. Mean wasn't so bad, but mean and smart were a bad combination.

He continued on over the harsh ground. It was mostly dust and rocks with patches of buffalo grass and, here and there, bunches of the tough mesquite weeds. Occasionally there were small brakes of greasewood brambles and beds of thorny mescal cactus, but there wasn't a tree in sight or a bush higher than a man's waist. As he approached the cabin, he was uncomfortably aware of just how empty the country was with not a sign of cover in sight.

A half mile short of the place he pulled up his horse and sat staring at the cabin. He had a packhorse on a lead rope. Both the horse he was riding and the pack-horse were thirsty and hungry and just about played out. If the cabin was occupied, there would be water and, perhaps, feed for his animals. But if it was, there would also be at least one very dangerous man inside. Maybe more than one. He had been on their trail for five days and the better part of two hundred miles.

His name was Custis Long, though most people referred to him as Longarm, and he was a deputy United States marshal. His base was Denver, Colorado, but his work took him wherever federal law felt the need of a man who didn't mind going into dangerous situations and setting matters right. At least that was the view that his boss, Billy Vail, took. Longarm wasn't so sure about not minding going into dangerous situations. He went, but it was not always with a high degree of willingness.

Now he sat his horse and studied the cabin. There was not a sign of life, but that didn't mean anything. If Jack Shaw was in there, he was perfectly capable of sitting as still as a stone until he had some reason to react.

Longarm wanted to see the other side of the cabin. If there was a corral it would be at the back, and he wanted to see if there were any horses present. He could, he knew, have safely made a big wide circle to come up behind the cabin, but he wasn't sure his horses could stand the extra work. It was June and it was hot. Long-arm thought it was as hot as the door handle on a whore-house. He could see little waves of heat shimmering off the prairie in every direction.

He figured the cabin was a line shack. In such poor country, where it took five hundred acres to feed one head of beef, ranchers erected such dwellings for their line riders. Cattle tended to drift toward the south, especially in the spring, autumn, and winter. It was the line rider's job to throw the cattle back up toward the north, driving them five or ten miles in that direction and then turning back to catch another bunch. The cabins were usually situated about fifteen miles apart down on the southern line of the property owner's land. More than likely there was another cabin to the west of the one he was looking at, and another to the east. At this time of year, summer, the cattle would be on the northern ranges, in the foothills of the mountains, where it was cooler. If the cabin was occupied now, it wouldn't be by a line rider.

Longarm felt as tired as his horses. His pursuit of the men who had robbed the train had been as relentless and hurried as the terrain and his horses would allow. He had slept only when it was forced on him by his body, and his meals had been snatched and incomplete. He had left the site of the robbery riding one horse and leading three others. Two he had turned loose as they had faded and failed, leaving them to make it on their own if they could in the rough, mountainous country he'd been through. Now he was down to just these two horses. More like one and a quarter, he thought grimly. He looked up at the sky, judging by the sun that it was about mid-afternoon, maybe earlier, maybe somewhere between two and three o'clock. He'd put his watch in his saddlebags for safekeeping. Some of the country he'd been crossing had been so rough and jumbled he'd expected the fillings to fall out of his teeth.

He sat, trying to figure out what to do. By his best calculations his locale was about seventy miles north of the Mexican border. The sign he'd struck as he'd come out of the last of the mountains had indicated he was close on to his quarry. If that was the case, then there was an excellent chance that the game he was hunting would be in the cabin.

But just how many of them there were, he could not

say. Which was one of the reasons he wanted to get a look behind the cabin and see the number of horses there. Of course that might not necessarily tell him anything. There might be five horses behind the cabin, but that didn't mean there'd be five men in the cabin. In fact Longarm felt pretty sure there wasn't but one. But if it was the one he thought it was, then one was more than a handful.

He reckoned it to be Jack Shaw. And he half hoped it would be, while another part of him hoped that it wouldn't be.

Jack Shaw was a former law officer gone bad. Longarm had known him for at least fifteen years, back when he, Longarm, was just getting comfortably settled into his role as a federal marshal and Jack Shaw was a man who specialized in pinning on a badge and cleaning up border towns. He'd become a legend, making things warm for outlaws in towns from Brownsville, Texas, clear on across New Mexico and up the border to Nogales, Arizona Territory, and on to Calixico, California. As far as Longarm was concerned, the Mexican border territory was about as bad as it got and to go in there as a town-tamer was seriously dangerous work. You had to be a hell of a hombre just to stay alive under such circumstances, much less hang and jail as many bandits as Jack Shaw had. Longarm had always wondered why a man would choose to work under such trying conditions. Jack Shaw had always said he simply liked it and it really wasn't as dangerous as it appeared. But then had come faint rumors about this prisoner escaping or that outlaw vanishing from a jail, and about Jack Shaw having more money to spend than seemed right. Finally, after nine years on the job, Jack Shaw had shown his true colors. He'd robbed a bank in Del Rio, Texas, in the very town where he was marshal, and had escaped with better than twenty thousand dollars. After that had come a succession of robberies in towns where Jack had worked as a sheriff or town marshal. In some cases he had been identified; in others it had only been speculation that he had been involved. He was tough, he was daring, and he knew the ins and outs of both sides of the law. All in all he made a formidable adversary. Longarm could think of any number of men he'd rather go up against if the objective was to get out alive.

He could feel his horse shudder under him, and he knew he couldn't stay put any longer. He wanted to get closer to the cabin and at the same time work around to the back. He urged his mount forward, feeling the pull of the packhorse behind. He rode obliquely, nearing the cabin but making one yard sideways for every yard forward. Finally he had the angle of the side and front wall facing him, and was just starting to see the posts of the corral behind the shack. He pressed forward. The distance between him and the cabin shortened. It came down from two hundred yards to one hundred, and then began to diminish so that he could see the scarred and weatherbeaten details of the shack. It had several windows, but they were small and not paned with glass. One or two had outside shutters, but they hung loose and askew, swaying just slightly with the very light breeze. There was a windmill just behind the cabin.

At a distance of about seventy-five yards Longarm was ready to conclude that the cabin was empty. He was able to see about half the corral, but he didn't see any horses. Of course they might be bunched up against the back of the cabin, seeking what shade there was.

All of a sudden he heard a thunk. Immediately there followed the report of a gun that sounded like a rifle. Longarm felt his horse stumble, and he knew the horse had been hit and was going down. He began, moving swiftly, to get ready to dismount. As rapidly as he could he unwound the lead rope from the saddlehorn so that the pack animal would be free. In the same motion he drew his carbine out of the boot on the right side of his saddle. His eyes were already searching the ground ahead for cover as he felt his horse go to its knees. He heard the buzz of a bullet near his ear and then the sound of the gun. With his carbine in his right hand, he was just able to grab his canteen by its strap and step onto the ground as his horse, with a gurgle and a sigh, fell forward onto the sandy prairie.

Stopping and weaving, Longarm ran forward, frantically looking for cover of any kind. Ten yards further on he saw a little wash. It wasn't much, no more than a little depression in the prairie floor some two feet deep by four feet wide by ten feet long. A little clump of greasewood clung to one end. Longarm lunged for the wash just as another bullet kicked up dust no more than a foot from his boot. He ran the last few yards and flung himself down, hugging the bottom of the wash as another bullet ripped through the air over his head.

For a moment he was content to lie still, doing his best to flatten himself out. He was lying almost lengthwise in the wash, with his head just slightly pointing toward the cabin. He'd managed to land behind a low fringe of the greasewood bushes, but there was a heavier thicket to his right. All of a sudden he realized he was still wearing his hat as another slug went whizzing just over his head. As deftly as he could, without raising so much as a shoulder blade, he eased his hat off and let it fall in the sandy, rocky clay of the wallow. Then, using the toes of his boots and his elbows, he worked himself along the edge of the wash until he'd reached the center of the greasewood bramble. The worthless plant had grown thick along the top part of the wash, a tribute to its ability to survive where nothing else could. At the base of the greasewood were little stalks of woody growth about an inch thick. They immediately curled up and onto themselves to form a tangled bramble. Sometime past it must have rained, allowing the plant to take good root and grow. Longarm could see it was starting to die, but he was grateful it had lasted long enough to give him what shelter it could.

When he thought he was in a good enough position, he lifted his head just enough to see over the edge of the wash and between the stalks of the greasewood. He seemed to be exactly at the corner of the cabin. He was facing one wall as much as he was facing the front of the little building. He studied the place closely, looking for a weakness. The cabin had been built of rocks, probably rocks that were handy nearby, and then chinked with adobe mud. There was no porch, and the roof might as well be called flat. As little as it rained in that country, there didn't appear to be any need for a pitch that would allow the water to run off. As near as he could tell, the roof was made of tin. He could see a good part of the corral and, yes, there was at least one horse in the back. All he could see was a tail and part of a rump. But if his man was in there he'd be well supplied with horses, ready for the last dash to the border and to Mexico.

A voice suddenly called out, "That you, Custis?"

Longarm lifted his head just enough to answer back. In the dry, thin air of the high prairie, sound carried a great distance. He had only to raise his voice slightly. He said, "Yeah, it's me. That you, Jack?"

"Yeah. How you been getting along?"

"Oh, pretty fair. How about you?"

"Can't complain. Pretty hot, I'd reckon."

"Well, it's that time of the year. What can you expect."

A bullet suddenly whipped through the greasewood, coming within a foot of Longarm's face. He dropped instantly flat against the dirt. Out of the side of his mouth he said, "Jack, I ain't gonne talk to you if you're gonna shoot at the sound of my voice."

He could hear a laugh. "Hell, Custis, you can't blame me. I don't reckon you've come for a social visit. I tell you, though, you can't trace sound up here the way you can on lower ground. I bet I missed you a yard or better."

"What you want to bet I ain't going to answer that."

Jack Shaw laughed again. "I'm right sorry about your horse, Longarm. I hate to kill a horse."

"You done that one a favor. He was about to founder under me. He'd already gone to trembling."

"Well, it's the way them damn heat waves shimmer.

7

Throw your aim off. I meant to take a shot at you, but you kept getting closer and closer and I couldn't chance it in case I missed. You might have made you a one-man cavalry charge right at the cabin. But I had to stop you. You can understand that.''

"You by yourself?"

Shaw said, "Well, I guess, like you said, I'll let you make a bet on that one."

"Can't see how there'd be many of you left."

Shaw said, "I see you tracked along right in my prints. That was a pretty handy piece of work. You know what's funny about this?"

"Naw."

"Wasn't a week ago I was talking about you. Right before we was gettin' set to do this job I told the boys, I said, I hope to hell Longarm is off somewhere else tending to something. He knows this here territory, and that hombre is the last man you want on your trail. Son-ofabitch don't give up.''

"Them is kind words, Jack. And you ain't that easy to trail. Of course you did slow yourself down by taking time out to kill off your gang. That must have been some slick doings, Jack, getting rid of the whole bunch."

"What makes you think I did? How you know they ain't two or three of us in here?"

Longarm eased an eye up over the edge of the wash, trying to figure out if the voice was coming from one of the windows or the open front door. He said, "Jack, I can still hear the sound of your rifle in my head. You know as well as I do that every gun has its own sound. If there'd been more than you in there, there would have been more than one gun shooting at me, and I didn't hear but the one."

"You reachin' for that one, Custis."

"Aw, Jack, don't come that on me. Ain't you ever been in a blind fight and figured out who was who and who was where by the sound of their individual weapons?"

"Yeah, but I thought I was the only one could do it.

8

I hate to hear it's all that common.''

"Oh, it ain't, Jack. You've gone and forgot you once explained that to me when you was the sheriff at Eagle Pass. I thought it was a bunch of whiskey talk until I taught myself to listen. Has come in right handy through the years. Like now.''

Shaw laughed. ''Well, I'll be damned. Just shows a man ought to know when to keep his mouth shut.'' There was a pause. ''Yeah, me and you go back a pretty good ways. I reckon we've drank more than a little whiskey together.''

"That we have, Jack. That we have.'' Longarm eased his head around and located his canteen. The strap was near his hand, and he pulled it to him and felt the two-quart flask. It was less than half full. He unscrewed the top and took just a little in his mouth to relieve the dry parching. A dry mouth made it hard to talk, and he didn't want Shaw catching on to how thirsty he was any sooner than necessary. He craned his head back a little further. His dead horse lay some fifteen yards away. It might as well have been fifteen miles. There was a big two-gallon canteen tied on the back of his saddle, and there was food and smokes and whiskey in his saddle-bags. He saw no way in the world to get to it with any certainty of living through the experience.

The packhorse had stopped a few hundred yards away and was standing, all four legs braced, his head down and the lead rope hanging to the ground. The horse really wasn't a pack animal. He was just one of the horses that Longarm had brought along that had been pressed into service for that purpose. On one side he was carrying a big sack of corn, feed for the horses, and on the other a twenty-gallon tin of water that Longarm had intended to use to water the horses as they'd entered the badlands. Unfortunately, the tin had bumped up against a rock and sprung a leak. It had emptied before Longarm had noticed. But it wouldn't have mattered. All the feed and water in the world wouldn't have saved the horses the way he'd been driving them.

Shaw said, "So you say you come across some unfortunate fellers fell upon a hardship?"

Longarm said, "Yeah, if your middle name is hardship, Jack. That must have been pretty slick the way you done them boys in one at a time without the rest of them getting wise along the way."

"Is that how you figure there's only me in here, by the count you took?"

"Well, they was eight of you to start with. One man got killed at the robbery by a foolhardy passenger. That left seven. I found two shot in the back a little less then a mile after ya'll rode into the Mescal Mountains when you was first getting away."

"Why you want to figure that was me? What makes you think we didn't draw some fire getting away from that train?"

Longarm said, "Aw, hell, Jack, now you are cutting up cute. Them two members of your gang was at least three quarters of a mile from the train, and there was uneven ground between them and the site of the robbery. Hell, Buffalo Bill, standing on top of one of them train cars, couldn't have made that shot with a Sharps .50-caliber on the best day he ever saw and the wind dead calm. Besides, both of them men was shot with a revolver. One of them was shot so close the muzzle blast damn near set his shirt afire."

Longarm could hear Shaw chuckle. "Well, I got to hand it to you, Custis. You are a hard man to fool. I ever tell you I used to admire you? Still do."

"Yeah, I used to admire you too, Jack."

"But not no more?"

Longarm thought a moment. "Well, we went in different directions. But it ain't so much that. Used to be you played pretty fair. But I can't say much for several cold-blooded murders back there. That clerk on the postal car. That was a shade on the mean side. Shot him to pieces little by little."

Shaw's voice came back, heated with indignation. "Now just a damn minute. That was Original Greaser

Bob's work. That clerk wouldn't open the safe for us. I was plannin' on twisting his arm or something that hurt pretty good, but next thing I knew Greaser Bob commenced to shooting the poor bastard in the elbow and the leg and the belly. I hated to see it and I wouldn't never have done it, but I got to say it impressed the hell out of the other clerk. Didn't take him no time to decide to open up that safe.''

"Was more than one killed there, Jack."

"I killed the passenger and I killed the fireman. And I wounded the engineer. But that was different. They was armed and was attempting to kill me. Hell, Custis, you know me pretty good.''

"I admit it didn't look like your style, Jack, but you never know—folks change.''

"I ain't changed that much and you can bet your last pair of boots on it.''

Longarm made a dry chuckle. "Way the situation looks I may be wearin' them.''

Shaw said, "Well, hell, ain't no use being strangers about this matter. I'm settin' here in the shade drinkin' whiskey. Whyn't you come on up and help me put a dent in this jug?''

Longarm said, "Guess you didn't hear, Jack. I quit drinkin'. Give it up.''

"Joined the Women's Christian Temperance Union, have you?''

"Took the veil." Back in his saddlebags, unless they'd been broken when his horse had fallen, were two quarts of the finest Maryland rye whiskey. It almost physically hurt Longarm to think how close they were and yet so far away. But he knew, as low as he was on water, it was no time to be drinking whiskey. Whiskey dried you out, made you more thirsty than you'd normally be. The whiskey would have to wait.

But then his overall situation wasn't of the best, at least not to his way of thinking. He pulled his rifle near him and looked to see if there was dirt in the barrel or the slide chamber. The carbine was a Winchester

.44-caliber lever-action model that was accurate up to about five hundred yards. It fired the same caliber cartridge as his revolver, which was a Colt with a six-inch barrel. He had an extra handgun of the same make and caliber, but with a nine-inch barrel. Unfortunately, it was in his saddlebags. It seemed that everything he could put to good use was in his saddlebags, including his extra ammunition. He knew he had six shells in his carbine and six in his revolver, and he knew, because it was his habit, that he had some extra cartridges in his shirt pocket, his right-hand pocket, the one he didn't carry his cigars and his matches in. Moving carefully, he reached his hand up and dug down in the pocket, hoping he'd been extra generous with himself. He tilted his chest forward and let the shells drop out in his palm. There were seven. He had a grand total of nineteen cartridges, and no way to get any more without getting shot about five times in the attempt.

He ran his tongue around his dry mouth and peered through the greasewood at the cabin. There was no movement of any kind, not even a shadow. Half reluctantly he took a brutal inventory of his situation. He was pinned down in a very precarious position against a man he knew to be smart, skilled, and willing. He was very low on ammunition, lower on water, and had no food whatsoever. He was exposed to a brutal sun, which would make his need for water all the greater, and help was a minimum of two or three days away, even assuming the help could find their way. He couldn't get to a horse, and even if he could, the animal wasn't fit to travel. Meanwhile, his adversary was in the shade, had food and water, not to mention whiskey, and was in a very defensible position. More than likely Jack Shaw was well mounted with spare horses to boot. Looked at from a realistic point of view, Longarm had to admit to himself that he really didn't have the best of it.

Shaw called from the cabin. "Longarm, that packhorse of yours is moving around."

Longarm looked over his shoulder. He could see the

poor animal staggering around aimlessly. Each time he tried to take a step he seemed to step on his lead rope. It jerked his head down and made the animal rear back in fright. One of the horses behind the barn nickered. The pack animal lifted his head and flicked his ears. Longarm heard a creaking. He looked toward the cabin. There was a little windmill behind the cabin, and enough of a breeze had sprung up to turn its rusty blades. It would be pumping water, and Longarm hoped the pack-horse would smell it and somehow get over to the corral. He said, "Jack, if that packhorse gets over your way, how about letting him in the corral so he can get some water?"

"Why don't you lead him over?"

"C'mon, Jack, this ain't something to fun around about."

"You must be funning around if you think I'm going to leave off watching you and go out the back of the cabin to let your horse in. I reckon when I come back I'd find you sitting in my rocking chair and drinking my whiskey and waiting to put a bullet in my belly."

"You know that ain't my style. I give you my word I won't move an inch if you can help the horse."

"Ain't worth the risk, Longarm. Not even as much as I think of you. Hell, I don't even trust myself that much."

Longarm swore. "Then goddammit, put a bullet through his head and put him out of his misery." The horses in the corral nickered again, and this time the packhorse answered them. Longarm saw him putting his head up, trying to smell, but the wind was wrong for him to scent the water.

Shaw said, "Why don't you put a bullet in him." There was a pause, and then Longarm heard Shaw chuckle. "Or be you low on ammunition? Seems I recall you never carried extra shells in your gunbelt. Said they were too heavy. I don't neither for the same reason, but then I got me several boxes full right here. I bet you got just what you bailed off your horse with when you flung

13

yourself down in that little ditch. You know I missed you on purpose, don't you?''

"You gonna bullshit me, Jack?''

"Hell, if I'd of killed you who would I have to talk to? I was getting lonesome till I saw you come out of those foothills way back yonder. I knew it was you when you wasn't no more than a speck.''

Longarm stared at the baked earth beneath his face and shook his head. He didn't want to think about it too severely at the moment, but he was pretty sure he should have handled the situation differently. If his horses had had one more mile in them, he'd have ridden around the cabin and looked it over from the rear. That way he'd have had Shaw boxed in, unless he cared to flee on foot, which wouldn't be very smart. Longarm wasn't sure if he was going to get out of the mess he'd gotten himself in, but he desperately dreaded having to write the report that would be due following the outcome. His boss, Billy Vail, who delighted in any stumbles Longarm made, would never let him forget it.

Shaw said, "Reason I mentioned about that packhorse of yours is that if he comes wanderin' over here and wants to get in a line between us, I'll have to drop him before he can do that. You be close enough now. I wouldn't care to have you come rushing forward and using the animal for cover.''

"Still thinking ahead, eh, Jack?''

"Never be as good at it as you are.''

"Yeah. That's why I'm in this ditch and you're in the shade.''

"Ain't gettin' hot, is it?''

"No, no. Fact is I was just wishing I had my ducking jacket. Getting a little chilly out here.''

He heard Shaw laugh. He could feel his shirt getting resoaked for about the third time that day. He reckoned the garment was mostly salt by now. A drop of sweat fell off his nose as he wiped his brow, trying to keep the salt out of his eyes. He glanced up at the relentless sun, trying to gauge how long until dusk. He said,

14

"What time you got, Jack?"

"Why, you got a train to catch?"

"Just curious. My watch stopped."

He could hear Shaw chuckle. Then the outlaw said, "I reckon you are calculating on how long it is to dark. I think you got it in your mind to maybe make some kind of play in the blackness. Well, friend Longarm, I'd chuck that one out the window. Gonna be moon bright. Moon going to be as full tonight as it gets. Going to be that way for two, three more nights. Hell, if you had one, you'd be able to read a newspaper be so light."

Longarm cursed silently to himself. "Well, I'm glad to have your word on that, Jack."

"What the hell you think I'm doing still here with the border no more than a day and a half away? Waiting for a dark night. I'd just as soon folks kept on looking for me around here instead of stirring up the Mexican authorities. You know that Mex law, Longarm. They don't give a damn about me, but if they get word about how much gold I'm carrying, they are likely to take a right smart interest. So I kind of planned to be just as quiet and easy when I cross on over. Sort of keep it my secret."

"Well, looks like we're going to have plenty of time for a good visit, Jack."

Shaw said, "Well, I don't know about that, Longarm. I got a look at the size of that canteen you was toting when you scrambled for that ditch. Even if it was full, which I doubt, you'd have a hell of a time making two days on that piddling amount of water. That sun will sweat the fluid out of you, Custis. I know. It'll draw it right on out like a whore suckin' the money out of your pocket. Or maybe suckin' something else out of you, if you take my meaning."

Longarm was quiet for a moment. Then he said easily, "Well, Jack, when you come right down to it, we might not have to wait long at all to settle this little question. You are sitting in there in a square rock cabin and I got a real good angle at two windows and a door. I got steel-

15

jacketed cartridges in this carbine, and it occurs to me I might go to letting some shots off through them windows and those steel slugs might get to ricocheting around and around in that little room and one of them might pass through your body. I know it ain't exactly precision shooting, but it's the best I can come up with under the circumstances.''

Shaw said, ''Aw, hell, Longarm, let me get these jeans off so you can pull my leg better. You ain't got the ammunition for that kind of play. You hit the ground with a pistol on your hip and a carbine in one hand and a canteen in the other. Unless you was carrying cartridges in that canteen, you got just what you've got loaded.''

Longarm waited a moment. ''You wouldn't care to bet your life on that, would you? You know, them cartridge heads get to flying off rock and sometimes they split apart and they'll be rock fragments flying. Might get a bit warm in there.''

Shaw laughed. ''I got to give you credit, Custis. You still ain't lost your touch. I bet you talked more men down in a fight than you ever gunned down. And it takes a man of your reputation—fairly earned, I might add— to do that. But there is one slight error in your plan. They is a root cellar in here and the first time you let fly, I am going to be down in it with a gun in each hand waiting for you to walk through the front door.''

Longarm thought a moment. His legs were starting to cramp up from the fixed position he'd been lying in. He didn't reckon he'd ever been so uncomfortable in his life. Then he said, ''You wouldn't be lying about that, would you, Jack?''

''No more than you're lying about your ammunition.''

They were both quiet for a time, thinking it over. Finally Longarm said, ''That whiskey making you sleepy, Jack?''

''Oh, no. No, no, no. I've had me a good rest. Got

16

here early last night and been sleeping and dozing ever since. How about you?''

''Oh, the same. Fact of the business I've had too much sleep.''

''Slept, did you, whilst you was trailing me?''

''Aw, yeah. Soon as I had you lined out, I just pointed the horse and relaxed in the saddle and slept most of the night away. In fact I overslept breakfast. Horse wouldn't stop.''

They were both quiet for a while. Then Shaw said, ''This is mighty good whiskey, Custis. Shore you won't have some?''

''Jack, you know what I reckon? I reckon we got us a standoff here. I guess you'd call it a Mexican standoff close as we are to the border.''

Shaw laughed. ''Now who be doing the bullshitting? Hell, Longarm, I can get on a horse and ride out of here anytime I'm of a mind.''

Longarm shook his head slowly even though Shaw couldn't see him. ''I wouldn't count on that, Jack. Not day or night. I got an angle on that corral and I would see you trying to slip off. You have seen me shoot. And like you said, I can make sure of it by shooting your horses. Naw, I wouldn't count on that.''

There was silence for a time. Then Shaw said, ''You know, Custis, all I got to do is go out that back door, climb up on the roof, and you will be in plain sight. Easy pickings.''

''Jack, that roof is flat as your first wife's chest. You show yourself up there and you gonna be the one in plain sight. Right over a pair of iron sights. I couldn't miss if I tried.''

Shaw said, ''Longarm, I am starting to regret you paying me this visit. Course we've got the night to go yet, and then tomorrow. And don't be too sure I can't get away from you while you are napping. I can lay up nearer to the border and be just as happy while I wait for a dark night.''

Longarm glanced at the sun again. If anything it

seemed higher in the sky. He felt as if he had been talking to Jack Shaw for the better part of the afternoon, but time just wouldn't seem to pass. He glanced over at the packhorse, who had moved a little nearer to the corral but had apparently not smelled the water. But now the little breeze had died and the windmill had stopped creaking around. He felt sorry for the poor old horse, but he didn't know what he could do. He couldn't waste a cartridge. He had few enough as it was.

He shifted around, trying to get more comfortable. The canteen was temptingly close to his hand, but he knew he dared not drink yet. He calculated he was in for a long siege. He yawned. It frightened him. To sleep was as good as a bullet through the head. But Lord, was he tired! He felt like he'd been dragged behind a stampede for a hundred miles. Every part of his body ached, and he had lied pretty much as big as it was possible to lie about the sleep he'd gotten. He reckoned in the last five days he hadn't amassed more than ten, maybe twelve hours total. It had been hard tracking as the outlaw gang had left one small range of mountains and cut over and picked up another one, all the time heading generally south. He'd wasted valuable time following false leads left by other men who'd passed through the same country, and lost ground and time climbing down into gullies to discover the bodies of the outlaws that Shaw had been slowly eliminating one after the other.

Shaw called out, "Hey, Custis! You ain't sleepin', are you?"

"Naw. Just wonderin' what kind of deal me and you can make. You give yourself up and I'll split the reward money the railroad is sure to put up on you."

"Tch, tch, tch. Custis, I'm ashamed of you, lying like that. You didn't used to carry on so. You and I both know that federal marshals can't collect reward money. What you want to go and tell me a whopper like that for?"

"Just passing the time, Jack. All I got to do."

"Whyn't you tell me how you tracked us? That'd

18

make pretty good listening.''

"Why don't you tell me how you managed to do away with that bunch so you'd have all the money to yourself without a couple of them getting wise somewhere along the line?''

"What are you talking about?''

"Your riding partners, your gang. The men you killed.''

Shaw laughed. "Why, listen to you, Custis. Next thing you'll be accusing me of robbing trains.''

"C'mon, tell it. Either you are slicker than I thought, or them was one dumb bunch of outlaws.''

The words were no more than out of his mouth than he heard the faint hiss of a bullet and felt the breeze as it passed just in front of his forehead. The hard crack of the rifle came right on the heels of the passing slug. Longarm ducked instinctively, drawing his revolver as he did, and edged an eye over the rim of the wash. Somehow Jack Shaw had gotten a better angle, found a higher position to allow him to aim down on Longarm.

His glimpse caught Jack Shaw just stepping down from a chair by the side of the door. Longarm shoved his revolver through the brush and fired as Shaw was jumping back. He saw the slug catch the leg of the chair, making splinters fly and jerking the chair out of Shaw's hand. He'd fired too quickly to have had any hope of hitting the outlaw, but he had to make the man understand he couldn't take too many liberties.

From the cabin he could hear Shaw laughing. "Hell, Longarm, ain't no use getting all upset. Yore hair looked like it needed parting. You didn't have to ruin my chair.''

Longarm said dryly, "I bet you got other'ns, Jack. But let me give you a piece of advice. Stay off of them. Man can get hurt standing on chairs. Especially around doors or windows.''

"I guess that means you ain't going to come up for a drink. Bad business, a man drinking alone.''

"Jack, if you'd like to give yourself up I reckon I

could be forced to take a drink. Just step on out the door with your hands in the air and that will settle everything.''

Shaw said dryly, ''I'd like to, Longarm, I damn shore would. But I got a idea you'd want me to go to that Crossbar Hotel in Yuma for more than a few years. Problem with that is some of the folks living there be ones I put there myself when I was on the other side of the badge. You can see my point, can't you? I reckon those folks might not treat me too kindly.''

Longarm glanced up as he noticed the packhorse slowly trudging toward the corral. He'd stepped on his lead rope so often that it had finally broken off at the halter. But Longarm could see that the load the horse was bearing was shifting toward the corn side. The water drum was empty on the other side, and the weight of the corn was gradually pulling the load down on one side of the horse's flanks. Soon enough it would spook the horse and he'd go to kicking at it. The result of that, as soon as the horse spooked, would be a broken leg or neck or both.

The little breeze had picked up again and the horse had sniffed the water. As he neared the corral, Longarm could see the horses inside come crowding over to the railing of the pen. He counted five horses. They all looked in good shape. Longarm guessed that the horses Shaw had driven hard had been turned loose when they'd played out. He watched as the packhorse came up to the corral fence. The horses inside pressed forward eagerly, reaching out with their muzzles to test and smell and identify this newcomer.

Shaw said, ''C'mon, Custis, tell me how you trailed us. That was a job of work you done. I never figured nobody could stay with our tracks the route I took. And how did you get onto us so fast? Hell, I didn't beat you to this cabin by much more than twelve hours, maybe fourteen. You must have been hell on quick at getting to the site of the robbery.''

Chapter 2

By the sheerest of coincidences, Longarm had been in Globe, Arizona Territory, when the wire had come into the depot that the train out of Phoenix had been robbed. Globe was about two hundred miles east of Phoenix, a mining and garrison town that had been a stopover for Longarm on his way back to Denver from a job in New Mexico. The wire had been sent by the conductor, who'd tapped into the telegraph line by the side of the track with his emergency sending device, getting out word that the train had been robbed some forty miles west of Globe and that the engineer and fireman had been killed. It turned out later that the engineer had not been fatally wounded, but then neither was he in condition to drive a train.

Longarm immediately commandeered an engine and a stock car from the railroad and bought four horses from a livery. There was an army post ten miles outside of town where he could have got more and better mounts, but he didn't have the time to spare. He had no help and no deputies. He was the only officer, outside of the U.S. Army, with total jurisdiction throughout the territory. The town marshal's authority extended no further than the city limits. The sheriff was the law only in the county where he'd been elected. It was for this very reason that the Marshal's Service had been created, and Longarm had set out solo without the slightest thought of seeking help.

What with one thing and another, four hours had passed by the time he reached the motionless train where the robbery had taken place. After that, more time had been wasted while he'd tried to organize the passengers and train crew into a manageable body that could supply him with information. The passengers were understandably excited and frantic, since some members of the gang had gone among them robbing them of small amounts of cash and what jewelry they'd had. Some of the women had been fondled and kissed, and more than one man had been clubbed with a revolver.

With patient questioning Longarm was finally able to get a picture of the gang. It took only a few descriptive words about the man who seemed to be the leader for Longarm to realize that he was dealing with Jack Shaw. His heart sank. Shaw was a handful, not only because he was tough and ruthless and intelligent, but because he'd been a lawman and could think like one. There was no question it was Shaw. The crew and passengers described a tall, spare man who looked, in the words of one passenger, "about as lean and hard as a skillet lid." That could have described a lot of men, but the clincher was the birthmark on Shaw's right cheek. It was a little bigger than a silver dollar, red in color, and roughly heart-shaped. More than one man had regretted calling Shaw Cupid or asking whose valentine he was. He had immediately drawn the conductor's attention by the businesslike way he'd gotten into the mail car and then into the safe. The conductor said, "He went at it like he knew what was in there, that we were carrying a payroll. That man had advance word that there was a good chunk of money on this train. I'd stake my life on it."

And more than one had. The bandits had attacked when the train had stopped for water at a regular stop along the way. The engineer and the conductor had been rash enough to draw their guns and fight. They hadn't

22

fought long, not against eight determined killers. After the outlaws had gotten the train stopped, Shaw and two other men had turned their attention to the mail car, leaving the rest of the gang to terrify the three coaches of passengers. At one point, when it appeared some of the women might be raped, the conductor had appealed to the man with the birthmark to intervene. He had, to the point of shooting at one of his own men and telling the rest in no uncertain terms that their job was to disarm the passengers and then to get outside and watch from defensive positions.

Longarm asked about the outlaw Shaw had shot. The conductor shrugged and said, "Oh, he wadn't hurt all that bad. But it had a salutary effect on the rest of that murderous bunch. They hopped to their jobs Johnny quick and no mistake."

But there had been a dead outlaw. The conductor thought that the engineer or the fireman had killed him. "I can't say," he explained. "The guns was goin' off like firecrackers. You never heard such a racket in your life."

The conductor was anxious to get his train into Globe and see about the wounded, several of whom were passengers. Longarm unloaded his horses, along with the provisions he'd thrown together hurriedly in Globe, and made ready to take up the trail. The small train he'd brought from Globe pushed forward and hooked onto the engine of the train that had been robbed. It would be slow going, but Longarm's train would have to back all the way to Globe towing the other one.

But before he left, Longarm had the conductor hook into the telegraph wire again. There was a troop of Arizona Rangers outside of Phoenix, and he had the conductor wire their commander details of the robbery and word that he, Deputy U.S. Marshal Custis Long, was taking up the chase and would try to leave sign along the way for them to follow. He told the Rangers to get to the site with all possible speed and follow him as best they could. He added, "Leader is Jack Shaw. Have reason to believe they will head south for Mexico, but can't be sure. Don't think it wise to try and intercept their line of flight as Shaw very smart and unpredictable. Suggest you begin at scene of robbery.''

After that there was nothing to do but take up the chase. He added such provisions and water as he could out of the train larder and the freight cars. It was an incomplete and unwieldy load, but speed was of the essence. So he took what he could, threw it on a horse, and got underway. It was vital that he stay on a hot trail. Once it cooled, Shaw could make off in any direction. Longarm had no doubt that his final goal was the Mexican border, but there was absolutely no way of telling at what point he'd choose to cross. Notifying the law along the border would do no good, since they would be looking for a will-o'-the-wisp who might go silently and invisibly in any direction.

Longarm rode away from the train, knowing he had already lost valuable time, but still hurrying all he could. A short distance into the crags and gullies of the foothills of the Mescal Mountains he found the first two bodies. Both had been shot in the back. One of them had been Original Greaser Bob. The other one Longarm didn't recognize, just as he hadn't recognized the outlaw who'd been killed at the train. That was another habit of Jack Shaw's. He seldom used the same men on consecutive holdups, or even the same men ever. Jack Shaw was a very careful and secretive man, and it was said that a lot of the men who went out on jobs with Shaw had a bad habit of never being seen again. More than one sheriff or deputy had been heard to comment that Shaw was doing more to clean up the country than when he was wearing a badge. There was even talk that Jack Shaw wasn't a man who liked to share, but just as quick as such word would get around, Shaw would pull a job with three or four partners and every one of them would swear by the man.

Longarm had been a full thirty hours tracking the gang through the Mescals before he'd broken out into clear country. For a few miles the sign was plain. The party, now reduced to five men, had been heading due south. Then, in a patch of rock, the sign faded. Longarm spent a frustrating three hours until he located the bunch heading east. Then they'd turned south again and entered the Santa Teresa mountain range. If anything, it was rougher going than the Mescals. He lost his first horse there, a little dun that he'd known was too soft from livery life to stand the kind of pace he'd forced it to maintain. He turned the horse loose and tried to herd him down into a little draw which appeared to have grass and water. The dun was frightened, but the off-the-trail excursion led Longarm to an interesting discovery. He found an outlaw known as Hank Jelkco. It surprised Longarm because the man was known to be a small-time cattle thief down along the border. Train robbery, as near as Longarm had heard, was a little out of his line. But the discovery of the body cut the party he was chasing down to four. Longarm had a pretty good idea that it was going to get smaller as it went along. Jack Shaw didn't like to share.

The killing of Original Greaser Bob had surprised Longarm because Greaser Bob Landrum had been one of the few men who had consistently ridden with Jack Shaw. Longarm could only conclude that he had outlasted his usefulness. Or maybe Shaw had gotten tired of the silliness. Greaser Bob wasn't called that because he was Mexican. At some point in the past he had gotten in the habit of staining his face and hands with walnut juice, made by boiling walnut shells in water, to make himself appear as a Mexican. But since he looked nothing like a Mexican, the skin coloring fooled no one. He'd picked up the name Original when others had tried the trick, hoping to have the authorities hunting for Mexican bandits while they washed off the stain and went on their way as gringos.

Halfway through the Santa Teresas he came upon a cold campfire with a dead man lying beside it. Longarm didn't know the man, but he recognized the three bullet holes in the man's chest. Beside him, on the ground, was a tin plate of beans. It didn't appear he'd been given time to take a single bite. Longarm figured that Shaw had either picked a quarrel with the man, or had convinced the others that their accomplice was planning to steal the booty and make off with it some night when they were asleep.

Longarm finally followed the trail out of the Santa Teresas with the weakest of his three horses beginning to fade. That worried him. In the mountains there had been water and good grass and he'd paused long enough, knowing what was coming, to let the animals build up as much strength as they could.

Out of the mountain range Shaw had taken another straight southerly course. It was not bad traveling except for the heat. There was grass and an occasional water hole, and Longarm snatched what sleep he could and rested the horses when he could, but he could tell, from the age of the sign, that he wasn't making up much ground. All the way, since he'd left the train, he'd been leaving his own sign for the Arizona Rangers. He'd broken limbs, and stacked rocks, and had even torn up a shirt and used strips of it to mark the way. But now, out on the flats of the high plateaus, all he could do was ride his horses in a circle every so often and hope the Rangers weren't blind.

Then Shaw had abruptly cut west and entered the Galiuro range, which wasn't so much mountains as a series of low mounds with deep gullies, sharp crags, and slash precipices. There was almost no growth through the badlands since most of the ground was rock. It was halfway through the rough country that his next horse came up lame. He turned the horse loose and set back in on the trail. At first, he'd been trading off riding the three strongest horses, using the fourth, the weakest, to carry the pack. Then he'd been down to two saddle mounts. Finally he was down to one. He'd been on the trail four days and four nights, and he didn't know if he could catch Shaw before he made it to the border.

Once out on the flat land again, the going appeared to be fairly easy. The trail, especially with the number of horses Shaw had, was relatively easy to follow. Leaving the Galiuro range, he had taken a southwesterly heading, just about what Longarm had expected he would do. Longarm was so confident of the trail that he made an early camp on the fifth night out, hoping to get a few hours' sleep. Then, sometime during the late night, a hurricanelike wind blew up, not uncommon in that high desert country, and by the first light of dawn, Longarm could see that all traces of Shaw and his crowd had been blown away. All he could do was go ahead on the last known course, follow it, and hope.

About noon his hopes were rewarded. The country had been descending. In a little grove of trees he found traces of a campfire, a lot of horse tracks, and the bodies of Shaw's last two henchmen. Both of them had been shot in the back.

Unfortunately, the camp had been made right at a rock-rimmed canyon. That Shaw had crossed it, Longarm had no doubt, but he could not find a single trace of sign or proof of Shaw's passage. He pushed on in the southwesterly direction, calculating that Shaw would want to cross the border in a long, lonely stretch between Nogales and Douglas. But it was a lot of country to find one man in, especially a man who had five horses to ride to Longarm's one.

He had no choice except to push his tired horses across the trackless waste, sharing with them what little water he had left in the big canteen, once he'd discovered the mishap that had befallen the big tin of water he'd been counting on. The corn helped some, but the horses were too thirsty to chew it good. Most of it fell out of their mouths.

Then, finally, he spotted the line shack and rode forward and into trouble. He'd found Jack Shaw, but Jack Shaw had found him in equal measure.

• • •

An hour had passed without conversation between them. Longarm had stayed alert, watching for any movement of the horses in the corral that would indicate Shaw was trying to slip out of the back and mount and ride south. Longarm didn't really expect him to make such a dumb play, especially in the daytime. If he tried it, his move would come at night, probably very close to dawn, when the moon would have been down for at least an hour and the sun was yet to come. The old expression that it was darkest just before dawn was a true one and useful.

Shaw said, breaking the silence, "Custis, you never did tell me how you come to get on our track so quick. Or is that a government secret?"

"Not if you'll tell me how you done in Hank Jelkco. He didn't have a mark on him."

"You found ol' Hank? Hell, I went to considerable trouble to roll him down in the bottom of a gully. What was you doing down in there?"

"Trying to drive a dumb horse that was played out down to grass and water. Lo and behold, there was ol' Hank, dead as a whore's hopes. He'd fetched up against a little sapling. How did he come to depart this life?"

"Aw, I strangled the sonofabitch. It was the first night we really made a camp to rest up. I had the watch and when the others was asleep, I just cranked my hands around his neck and squeezed. He never even made a gurgle. Then I drug him over to that draw and rolled him off. Told the boys the next day that it appeared he'd taken a sack of money when my back was turned and lit out."

"And they believed that?"

Shaw laughed. "Custis, ain't you never noticed I don't pick the boys that go to the head of the class to ride with me? All I want them there for is to give anybody with a gun a choice of who to shoot at. Cuts down the odds on me being the one selected. I was holding the loot and wasn't a one of them knew how much we had, so they didn't know if there was any

28

missing or not. You got to remember, these boys are a mite on the selfish side. Hank was just one less to share with.''

''What about his horse?''

''I said it appeared he took off on foot, which was smart. Make him harder to trail. I said ol' Hank could go for days on foot. They didn't know one another, so they'd believe anything. Now how about you?''

''I was in Globe when ya'll done the deed.''

He could almost see Shaw shaking his head back and forth. ''Well, that was a bad piece of luck. If I'd known you was that handy I'd of give the whole thing up. But how'd you know about the holdup? We was forty miles from Globe.''

Longarm smiled to himself. He knew what he was about to say would irritate the hell out of Jack Shaw. ''Conductor got up one of them telegraph poles and hooked in and sent a message. I got it within an hour.''

There was a momentary silence, and then Jack Shaw's voice came back, stunned and indignant. ''You tellin' me the damn telegraph line wasn't cut!''

Longarm chuckled quietly to himself. He too had been surprised, especially when he had discovered that Jack Shaw was the leader. ''Shore as hell wasn't, Jack. That's how come I'm here.''

Shaw started cursing. Longarm estimated that he went on for a full two or three minutes without repeating himself. Longarm considered it a pretty fair exhibition of offhand swearing with no preparation. Finally Shaw ran down. He said, ''That damn Hank Jelkco got off way too light. That was *his* job, his job especially. Instead he got mixed up in that bunch that was robbing the passengers of nickels and dimes and jewelry. Kissin' women and such. Well, I'll be a sad sonofabitch!'' Shaw was quiet for a moment. Finally he said, ''Lord, I wish I had him to kill all over again. I damn well guarantee you I wouldn't strangle him in his sleep. No, sir. I'd roast the sonofabitch over a slow fire. Damn! Damn, damn, damn!''

Longarm said, "Well, Jack, I know how you must feel, but it was your job. You go to leaving them important details to somebody else and you see what can happen."

"When you're right you're right, Longarm. I guess I ought to be kicking myself. Hell, I normally wouldn't even let an idiot like Hank Jelkco steal a horse with me, but after Greaser Bob he was about the smartest hand I had."

Longarm whistled. "You was just about out of help."

"Longarm, you wouldn't believe the sad quality of folks you can find in this line of work. Did you notice that kid that was laying near Greaser Bob?"

"Yeah, but I didn't recognize him."

"He was a farm boy from Oklahoma. Never done nothing like this before in his life. The only thing he'd ever held up was his hand in school to get permission to go outside and take a piss. That'll give you some idea of what things have come to."

Longarm frowned. "That don't sound right, Jack. There's plenty of good guns along the border."

Shaw laughed. "Oh, the border. Hell, yes, the border. But do you reckon I'm going to be going down there and hanging round recruiting a bunch of folks? Hell, Longarm, don't talk like you got a cornbread ass and a watermelon mouth."

Longarm nodded as if Shaw could see him. "Yeah, I reckon you're right. You are a little too well known down in those parts to be spending much time."

"See, it's all right for you. You play a lone hand. You ain't got nobody to fault or praise but yourself. And don't think I don't envy you that. If I could get away with it, that's exactly the way I'd operate."

Longarm chuckled softly. "Well, I don't know, Jack. Right now I wouldn't mind having a few extra hands placed round that shack of yours. I figure we could make it pretty warm for you."

"I can't get over you riding up here like that. I

nearly couldn't believe my eyes when I had you in my sights."

"What would you have had me do, Jack? Camp out there a half mile off and wait? What if this cabin had been empty. I'd of looked like a damn fool. I've already told you I didn't have a pound of horseflesh left."

"You got smokes?"

"Yeah, but not many."

"I got plenty in here. Them little packages of Mexican cigarillos. Didn't you used to smoke them at one time?"

"You know me, Jack. I'll smoke a lariat rope if it's got any age on it and at least been cured in the sun."

"Well, ain't no need of you savin' yores. I'm a pretty good chunker. I reckon I could land one of these little packs in yore ditch if it come to need. I don't like to see a man suffer. Go ahead and light up."

Longarm tried to make his voice sound a little hoarse. "Tell you the truth, Jack, my mouth is full of cotton. I reckon I better quit talking for a while and maybe work up a little spit. Smoke don't taste so good on a dry mouth."

Shaw laughed wryly. "Plenty of water in here, Custis. Welcome to come on in and help yourself."

Longarm didn't bother to answer. He was working himself around to where he could hang an eye over the edge of the wash and have a good view of the cabin. But he had to find a position he'd be comfortable in because he had an idea he'd have to be able to hold it for quite some time. He kept easing around, moving his body slightly this way and that, until he found a position that allowed him to rest his face on a little hump in the front wall of the wash and still be able to peek over the edge and see the cabin through the roots of the greasewood brambles. He had carefully placed his revolver right next to his head, and now he reached back and gingerly drew his carbine up to his side where it was instantly handy.

After that he rested a few moments, making sure

31

he was in a comfortable enough position that he wouldn't have to move for at least a half an hour— longer if necessary.

As he carefully worked a small cigar, along with a match, out of his left-hand shirt pocket, he wondered if Jack Shaw really thought he was that dumb. Well, he thought, he would soon find out. He took a quick glance toward the cabin, then ducked his head down into the ditch, striking the match with his thumbnail as he did. In a second he had applied the flame to the little cigar, taken a hard puff to get it burning, and then quickly extended it to his left as far as his arm would reach, laying the cigar down. The smoke was just starting to curl upward from the burning end of the cigar as he got his face back on its resting place and his eye focused on the cabin.

He calculated that the smoke had risen no higher than a foot in the air when three slugs came slamming into the rear bank of the wash, cutting dirt off the leading edge and going right through the smoke. The *crack, crack, crack* of the rifle boomed loud in the thin air. Longarm was able to see that Shaw had fired around the edge of the door, the near edge, which did not expose his body. Almost as soon as the last blast of the rifle had reached his ears, Longarm let out a faint, but what he hoped was a believable, groan. Then he went very quiet, almost willing himself not to breath. His left eye, peering just over the edge of the wash, was glued on the front and the side of the cabin.

Some time passed. Longarm had no idea how much, except the sun seemed to suddenly get hotter and he developed an itch right between his shoulder blades. It was agony to just lay there, unable to twitch so much as a muscle.

After what seemed forever Jack Shaw said tentatively, ''Longarm? Longarm? Custis?''

Longarm lay motionless, almost afraid to breathe. There was no sign of movement from the cabin, not even a head stuck quickly around the door and then pulled back.

A few more minutes passed and Shaw said, "Aw, c'mon, Longarm. I was jest funnin' with you. Them slugs never went within ten feet of you. Now quit hoorahin' me. Speak up, man. Ain't you had enough time to work up enough spit to talk?"

Longarm couldn't be sure, but he thought he detected a note in Shaw's voice suggesting a fish who was thinking about taking the bait. But until something happened, all he could do was cling to the front face of the wash and watch, almost unblinking. Longarm was acutely aware that if his chance came, and it was a long shot in more ways than one, he'd have the smallest portion of a second to make his play. And he knew he'd be stiff and slow-moving from lying in one position so long.

Shaw said, his voice more urgent, "Aw, cut it out, Custis. Hell, I was jest funnin' around with them shots. You layin' in there playin' possum an' waitin' for me to bite. Well, I ain't gonna do it. So you go ahead and see how long you can lay still and not move or talk. Meanwhile, I think I'll have me a drink of whiskey."

By cutting his eye to the left, Longarm could see one of his last cigars slowly burning up without him getting a puff. A full inch of ash was showing. And the itch had moved until it was now down in the small of his back. Pretty soon, he reckoned, his leg would go to cramping up.

All of a sudden there came a flurry of shots whipping dirt up on the front edge of the wash and clipping through the greasewood. One of the shots hit so close to Longarm's face that it would have knocked dirt in his eye if he hadn't shut it just in time. Longarm reflected that the shots were too accurate to have been fired from a pistol, at the distance the cabin was. He guessed that Shaw had fired and reloaded as fast as he could work the lever of his rifle. It had been an impressive display, and served to remind Longarm that he was fooling with a seriously dangerous and competent man. And intelligent.

But Shaw had something else that made him far more dangerous. Or better yet, he was missing something. Longarm knew there was a word for it, but he couldn't call it to mind. Shaw didn't seem to care about anything, especially the wrong or right of matters. He just flat didn't seem to have a conscience of any kind. Longarm had heard it said of some men that they'd ''as soon shoot you as look at you.''

Jack Shaw was the only man he'd ever met whom he felt that was completely true of. And yet Shaw could be just as good company as a man could want. Longarm had had many a drink with him, many a conversation, maybe even shared some of the same women. But Shaw didn't seem to have what most people had inside them, something that told him when he'd come to a stopping place.

Longarm could feel his left shoulder start to cramp, and there was another itch developing at the back of his head. The sun burned down hotter and hotter. The packhorse was still standing near the corral fence, his head getting lower and lower. Maybe the night would bring the animal some relief, Longarm thought. Maybe it would bring *him* some relief. One of them damn sure needed some.

Longarm could feel his tongue sticking to the roof of his mouth. He wasn't even sure he could open his lips without pulling skin loose. He was also beginning to wonder how much longer he could last. When he'd chosen the safest and most comfortable position, it had seemed fairly restful. He had his whole body, down to his boots, pressed up against the front slant of the wash, with just his head and neck turned back to the left to watch the cabin. As the minutes passed, another muscle in his body began to cry out for relief. Pretty soon he'd be so sore and stove up that Shaw could just walk out and beat him to death with the end of a rope. He'd known, when he'd put the plan in action, that it was going to be a waiting game of long duration, but now he wasn't sure if it was worth the risk. He hadn't had a sip of water in well over two hours, and he knew he was getting badly dehydrated. The only way to use what little water he had was to space it carefully over the time he'd calculated he was going to have to wait. To go too long without water was as foolish as drinking it all at once.

Shaw said, "Now look what you gone and made me do, Custis. Waste ammunition. You know a man in my position ain't supposed to be doing that. I got plenty, but you can't never have too much. Why don't you quit playin' possum and let's have a little talk. Tell you what. I got a two-gallon canvas bag of water here I'll sling over to you if you'll ask for it. All you got to do is ask and it's yours. Now, what do you say? You know I'd keep my word on something like this, Custis. Me and you was good friends a long time. I wouldn't treat you like that worthless trash I have to use to get my living." He paused. "Say somethin', Custis, an' I swear I'll sling you this bag of water."

Longarm lay still and gritted his teeth. Shaw had to be curious. He wouldn't be human if there wasn't some hope in his mind that he had hit Longarm, hit him and killed him. Shaw had suggested the whole business about the cigar with the idea in mind of getting Longarm to expose himself with the smoke. A man of Jack Shaw's vanity would almost have to believe he was right. At least that was the way Longarm had it reasoned out. Now all he needed was for Shaw to act like he was supposed to. If Longarm couldn't believe in the success of his own scheme, what could he believe in?

Shaw said, "Custis, if you don't show yourself I'm gonna go on out back, get me a horse, and ride for the border. I know you ain't got nothing wrong with you except you eat too much hair pie. Now sing out 'fore I ride off taking all the horses and leave you to bleach in the sun."

Longarm was not at all worried about that threat. Before Shaw would put himself on a horse on the open prairie, he'd make sure Longarm was either dead or unable to use a rifle.

It grew quiet again. Longarm now had cramps in three muscles and at least four distinct itches. His mouth was so dry he could almost feel his tongue swelling to fill up the whole cavity. He wondered if he dared move enough to sneak a sip out of his canteen. The thought of the water in his mouth was like a torment, a temptation he wasn't sure he could resist much longer.

Then, just as he was about to give up, he caught a slight movement at the far corner, the furthest front corner of the cabin to his left. It wasn't much, just a flash of motion at the corner down near the ground. Longarm figured Shaw had taken a very quick peek to see how much distance he'd have to cover to get close enough to the wash to look down and discover what condition Longarm was in.

After that nothing happened for a few moments. Longarm kept his eye riveted on the corner. When it seemed he could stare at the corner no longer, he saw Jack Shaw take a cautious step out into the open. He was holding a rifle with both hands, but he had a revolver shoved into his belt. He was perhaps fifty to sixty yards away.

As Longarm watched and held his breath, Shaw took a step. Then he stopped and glanced back as if to reassure himself that cover was near. He took another step toward the wash, and then another. His line of approach was taking him at an angle from the corner, an oblique approach pointed straight toward where Longarm lay watching.

Shaw took two more steps and then stopped. He put the rifle to his shoulder, sighted down its length, and swept the muzzle up and down the length of the wash. Longarm was becoming uncomfortably aware of how close Shaw was getting. In a few more steps he'd be able to see into the wash.

Shaw lowered the rifle and took two more steps. Longarm calculated he was no more than thirty to forty yards away. The land Shaw was standing on was slightly higher than the land around the wash. It gave him an advantage.

Longarm steeled himself, willing his muscles to be ready to spring into action. He knew he would have to use the carbine. It was far too long a shot for his revolver, especially since it was the one with the short barrel. Shaw started to take another step and Longarm knew it was time. In as fluid a motion as he could make, he rose from the wash, going to one knee, bringing up his rifle, and cocking it as he did. He had been afraid to cock it before for fear that the noise would alert Shaw. It seemed to take him forever to swing the rifle up to his shoulder.

Shaw's face briefly registered surprise and then an instant of confusion. But that passed quickly. It was clear he didn't have time to get his own rifle in firing position. In a single move he whirled and began running for the safety of the corner of the rock shack. He'd been twenty yards away from the cabin when Longarm had suddenly risen up out of the wash. By the time Longarm got the rifle to his shoulder and cocked it Shaw was within twenty feet.

Slowly Longarm tracked the fleeing figure with the muzzle of his rifle. Slowly his rear sight and front sight lined up. They were aimed directly at the small of Shaw's back. It was the biggest target because Shaw was running hunched over.

When Shaw was within eight to ten feet of the corner of the shack, Longarm slowly squeezed the trigger.

There was a faint click. There was no explosion, there was no gunshot, there was no bullet whizzing through the air to strike Jack Shaw in the small of the back and knock him flat.

Longarm did not know what had happened, but he dropped instantly back into the ditch. He worked the hammer of the carbine back and forth near his ear. He could hear the sound of grit. He ejected a shell, catching it in the palm of his hand, and looked at the end where the firing cap was. There was a very faint indentation on the edge of the rim-fired shell. He cursed silently and long to himself. Grit and dirt had gotten into the working parts of his rifle, enough to slow the hammer down so that it didn't strike the cartridge cap with enough force to explode the cartridge. He felt stunned, heartsick. He said softly, "Son of a bitch." He knew he'd never get a better chance. All that effort, all that discomfort, all that patience, all for nothing.

From back inside the cabin Shaw said, with a laugh in his voice, "You got to load them things, Custis, else they don't work worth a damn."

Longarm levered all six shells out, working to free the hammer and firing pin. As best he could he blew into the mechanism, hoping he had cleared it out enough that it would work. It had been just the worst kind of luck—there was no other name for it. Longarm had dragged rifles through the dirt for a hundred yards and they'd never misfired. Until now. He rolled back over against the face of the wash and began reloading his rifle. He said, "Naw, Jack, it was loaded. Must have been some dust or dirt got in the firing mechanism."

"That will happen to you in the desert. Course I'm kind of glad it did. You had me cold."

"Yeah, I shore thought so."

"Got to give you credit, Custis. You suckered me on that one. I'm a lucky duck to be all in one piece. Don't believe I'll be trying any such tricks on you again anyways soon."

Staying as low as he could, Longarm reached over and got the stump of the cigar. It had gone out. He had no plans to relight it, but he carefully put it back in his shirt. He said, "Well, Jack, you'll be glad to know that little stunt cost me half a cigar. I reckon that will go on your bill."

"Be glad to pay it, Custis. Why don't you step on up to the pay window right now."

Longarm had carefully loaded his rifle so that the shell that had not fired was in the chamber. He carefully worked the hammer back, dulling the *clitch-clatch* sound it made as he cocked it slowly. When the rifle was ready to fire he took a cautious look over the edge of his hole. There was no sign of Jack Shaw. Longarm would have liked to have had at least a boot toe to shoot at, but there was nothing. Next he glanced toward the packhorse. To his amazement the horse had somehow stretched his neck over the fence, bending the top board of the corral as he did, until he had managed to get his muzzle into the huge barrel that caught the water pumped up by the windmill. Apparently the few light breezes that had sprung up had been sufficient to fill the barrel to the brim so that the packhorse was able to just reach some moisture with his lips and suck it down. Longarm envied him. He took another careful swig out of his own canteen, being judicious and stingy with himself. The night might not be so bad, but the next day, he knew, was going to be hell.

Glad now that he didn't feel the need to kill the packhorse, he readied himself to test his rifle. He was able to draw his legs up without exposing himself so that he could come to his knees quickly. He took one more peek to make sure his enemy was not visible, and then came up swiftly and fired at the window. The hammer fell, the firing pin worked, and the bullet exploded. He was already facedown back in the wash as he heard the bullet go into the cabin and the whine and sing as it ricocheted around the inside walls of the rock shack.

He heard Shaw let loose with a volley of oaths. It didn't last long. Finally Shaw said, "What the hell you reckon you be doing?"

"Hell, Jack, I had to test my rifle, didn't I?"

"Yeah, but you didn't need to shoot in here. One of them goddamn rock splinters hit me in the ear and cut it. Dammit, you've drawed my blood."

"They say a good bleeding clears a man's system out, Jack."

"Yeah, well, I can do without no such foolishness. Hell, if you was going to waste a shell, how come you didn't shoot that damn packhorse you was so worried about?"

"Now, Jack, you know that would have caused me to expose myself while I took careful aim. If you'd seen me like that, I reckon there would have been more than the horse got taken down."

The sun was starting to flatten itself on the horizon. It would be dark soon, but it was no less hot for all of that. Longarm knew, of course, that sometime after midnight it would commence to get cold, and not just cold but freezing. That was the damned high prairie for you. Roast in the daytime and freeze at night.

Shaw said, "Be dark pretty soon."

"Yeah."

"I reckon to give you a little trouble tonight, Longarm."

"Aw, yeah, how's that?"

"Nothing you can't handle. Man like you."

"Well, what is it?"

"You're a gambling man. At least you were. You still of the same bent?"

"I still play at cards now and then if the stakes ain't too high."

"Stakes gonna be mighty high this time, Custis, mighty high."

"Tell me about it. I ain't got nothing else to occupy my mind."

Chapter 3

"Well," Shaw said, "it's a pretty simple little game. Sometime before dawn I'm going to open the corral gate. You can't see that from where you are. And some of these horses are going to get out. I'll make sure you hear that. Now the game for you is going to be to decide if I'm on one of them horses, riding off and making my escape, or not. Maybe I'm just running the horses out of the corral and then waiting for you to jump out of your hidey-hole and run toward the back to see if that is me waving adios to you. See the game?"

Longarm thought about it. It had actually been worrying him most of the day. He had wished his position had been much more to the side of the cabin so that he could see all of the corral. As it was, he figured he only had a view of not quite half, and the gate was obviously on the other side. All that day he had subconsciously studied the terrain, looking for someplace he could run to that would give him protection where he could see the side of the house and the corral. But the land had been flat as a griddle cake, with not even a semblance of a place to hole up. His only chance had been to shoot the packhorse, but the animal had not stayed in the proper position long enough. The horse he'd ridden in on was too far back, and would have afforded him no better view than he had. Shaw was right. It was a very chancy proposition. If he thought Shaw was making a break and left cover to stop him, Shaw could be still in the cabin with a rifle trained his way. And of course, the other side of that coin was that Shaw might *really* be riding off. If he did, Longarm would have no way to catch him. He'd make the border easily. Longarm was glad now that he hadn't mentioned anything about wiring the Arizona Rangers to Shaw.

Longarm said, "You ain't going to open that gate and let your horses out, Jack. You'd be crazy."

Shaw let out a whoop of laughter. "Longarm, I thought you knew a little something about cayuses. How far you reckon these old ponies are going to go away from this water? Hell, I'll probably have trouble keeping them out long enough to fool you."

He was right, Longarm thought. Shaw could drive the horses out of the corral, but they wouldn't stay out long. He said, "You got a point, Jack. But that old knife cuts two ways. If I tell you right now I'm going to take the bait, you ain't going to know whether to believe me or not. So that means you won't try to break out tonight. And if I'm convinced of that, then I won't show myself. But if you are of a mind to try it, it might be you chewing up some of this prairie. Might be a gamble either way you look at it."

Shaw laughed softly. "Got to hand it to you, Custis, you still play a hell of a hand of poker."

All of a sudden it was night. For just a little while it was dark, and then the biggest, roundest, most golden, brightest moon Longarm had ever seen filled the sky and threw light and shadows everywhere. You really didn't see it back in the valleys and draws of the mountains, not even when you were topping out on the terrain, because there was no flat horizon to judge it by. It was awesome. Longarm said, "See what

42

you mean about the moon, Jack. Unfortunately, I ain't got no paper to read.''

Shaw said, ''You probably got a better view of it. I'm fumbling around in the dark here trying to make my supper. All I got is dried beef and biscuits and cheese and canned peaches. I don't reckon you're hungry, though.''

''I ate earlier,'' Longarm said. ''Say, I still don't understand why you felt it was necessary to go through three batches of mountains. You switched your trail enough almost made me dizzy. You'd have been a lot better off, once you come out of the Mescals, making straight for the border. Instead you wasted four days rummaging around in that rough country.''

Shaw chuckled. ''Well, I tell you, Longarm. It's considerably easier to get rid of folks you don't want tagging along in tangled country. You can't do 'em in quite as easy out in the open, if you get my drift.''

Longarm shook his head. ''I ain't never goin' to understand how them boys let you knock 'em off one at a time. Was they that dumb or that easy?''

''Greed, Longarm. Plain old simple greed. Most of 'em knew I was picking off the weak ones, except for the first two they thought was brought down by fire from the train. But the rest of 'em, each one of 'em, thought they was gonna be the one I'd share the proceeds with. Remember them last two? Looks like I shot both of them, don't it?''

''Yeah, shore as hell does.''

''Wasn't the way it was. I told each of 'em to kill the other. One shot the other in the back and I done him the same favor. Greed, Custis, plain ol' greed.''

''Well, what I don't understand, Jack, is how come you didn't want to share none of it. Did you get so much you figured it was one big score and you was through? Or was it so little wasn't enough to go around?''

''You don't know the amount of the proceeds?''

"Naw. That was Indian Affairs money you got. Money was meant for the reservation people to buy supplies and whatnot. The folks on the train didn't have no idea how much money was in them sealed sacks."

Jack Shaw said, "Now you starting to get some idea about why I feel like the loot by rights belongs to me. All them men figured it was going to be share and share alike. But wasn't a man among 'em knew about that money being shipped to the Bureau of Indian Affairs out of Phoenix to Globe. Wasn't a one of them knew what train it was gonna be on. Wasn't a one of them knew within a thousand guesses how much money it was. And wasn't a one of them spent a week riding that track to figure out the best place to take the train and then another week riding the countryside to figure out the best escape route."

"And they seen it as an eight-way split?"

"Damn shore did. Was the only way they'd sign on. Hell!" Shaw made a disgusted sound. "Can you blame me? Hell, ever'body wants something for nothing these days. Man don't want to work for what he gets. I spent nine hard, dangerous years learning the law from the other side of the badge before I went the other way with that robbery in Del Rio. I earned my wages. But these punks these days, hell, they don't want to learn. They damn shore don't want to work. But they want a share. Oh, yeah, they expect theyselves a share. Well, I give 'em their share all right."

"You still ain't told me what amount of proceeds you got."

Shaw laughed, a short brittle sound. "I reckon I'll let you find out that for yourself. I will say I didn't get as much as the Indian Bureau will say they lost."

Longarm was quiet for a moment, thinking about it. Then he said, "Your inside man take his cut out first? Before he shipped the money?"

Shaw didn't answer the question. Instead he said, "Now, we might talk about giving you a share, Custis.

44

I know you probably won't take it, but I'm willing to leave five thousand—no, make that ten thousand—outside the front door in return for you taking a nap for about two hours.''

Longarm brought his carbine closer to hand and said, "Go ahead, set it on out there. Just outside the door.''

Shaw laughed his brittle laugh again. "Now, Custis, ain't no use in getting your feelings hurt. Hell! I had to make the offer. I shove any money out there it will be with a broom handle. Now if I've made you mad with my little proposition, then I apologize. I didn't mean nothing personal by it, and I don't see no point in me and you making anything personal about this situation. We are both professionals and I'm willing to act like it.''

"You still ain't told me why the Indian Affairs Bureau is going to report more of a loss than you took.''

Longarm could hear Shaw sigh. Then the outlaw said, "Well, just figure they don't count so good and leave it at that. I don't know what you mean by me having an inside man. I just overheard a conversation in Phoenix, that's all.''

"Nevertheless," Longarm said, "when this is over, I think I'll have me a look inside that Bureau in Phoenix. See if they is anybody there with a connection to you.''

Shaw said, his voice cool, but with a hardness in it Longarm had not heard before, "What makes you think you'll be getting out of this in the kind of shape where you'll be asking anybody anything?''

"Well, let's just say I'm hoping. How does that sound, Jack? Ain't that what you're doing?''

"I don't see why we can't make some kind of deal, Custis. I got the best of it right now. Even you got to admit that. But I'm still willing to talk about a deal. If you think today has been hard on you, why, you wait until tomorrow is good and settled in. You are fixing to find out how bacon feels when it's frying.''

Longarm said dryly, "This ain't my first county fair, Jack. Why don't you save that kind of hominy-grits talk for them as will buy it. You might get in short supply you waste it on me."

"Ain't no use gettin' testy, Custis. Gonna be a long enough night as is."

"Thought you was leavin'."

Shaw chuckled. "I'll let you get in a nap first. I know you got to be mighty tired for a man of your age. What are you anyway, Custis, 'bout forty?"

"Not for ten years yet. Question is, will you *git* to be forty?"

"You ain't much older than me and I just barely turned thirty-five."

"Come on out here and I'll whisper it in your ear."

"Fact of the business is, Custis, I don't really care a damn. Not that much anyway. Just being sociable. But I reckon I better quieten down now so you can get a little sleep."

The moon was well up. It was amazing to Longarm how light it was. It was, of course, a different kind of light from the sun. The shadows looked odd, mis-shapen and distorted, and the colors of things were all wrong. What was brown, like the shack, looked reddish, and the whitish parts of the prairie seemed to almost glow and shimmer. A faint breeze had come up, and Longarm could hear the rusty windmill blades creaking around. Looking to his right, he could see the packhorse with his neck stretched out, his head reaching, his lips sucking as he kept taking in water.

It was cooler now, but not all that much. Longarm calculated that it was somewhere between eight and nine o'clock, but he had no real way of knowing. He halfway wished that Jack Shaw had not stopped talking. Now that matters had settled down, he could feel just how tired he was. His body ached and cried out for rest; not just being stationary, but real rest, sleep rest, relaxed rest. He was lying down, but he wasn't resting. His whole body was tensed, alert for any sign

46

of action from the cabin. He shook his head and blinked his eyes several times. He could tell that it was going to be a long night. He looked to the right and wished feverently he had a position just twenty or thirty yards in that direction. It would make the job that much simpler. As it was, he couldn't say what he'd do if he heard Shaw's horses coming out of the corral. It would be a fifty-fifty risk. If he was right, he would shoot Shaw. If he was wrong, Shaw would shoot him. He stifled a yawn and glanced up at the moon. A few small clouds were passing across its face, and it was odd to see them reflected on the ground, dark patches moving blackly across the white and tan prairie. They looked like moving pools of water. He shook his head again and blinked hard. His canteen was at hand, and he picked it up and hefted it. There was no more than a quart left. He reckoned it would see him through the next day, but not by much. Tomorrow would be the day to start threatening Shaw with the Arizona Rangers. If he'd done it too soon it would have made Shaw that much more dangerous, and the man was too mean and too ingenious and too cunning to be pushed into a corner. For the time being let Shaw think that Longarm was all he had to worry about. So long as he thought that was the case, he'd be content to wait Longarm out, sure in the knowledge that the sun would do his work for him.

Longarm yawned and began to cast about frantically in his mind for something to think about that would keep him awake. Molly Dowd came floating toward him like the best dream he'd ever had.

Molly Dowd was the widow of a deputy marshal who had been one of Longarm's best friends, Tom Dowd. When Tom had been killed in a battle with road agents, Longarm had gone to the funeral, and then had stayed on to see what he could do for Molly. She had decided to remain in the same house that she and Tom had lived in, in a town in north Texas, Wichita Falls,

47

just below the Oklahoma Territory, which had been Tom's major responsibility.

One day, a year after Tom's death, a letter came to Longarm from Molly, inviting him to look in on her whenever he was close by. He thought of it as no more than a friendly invitation from a woman who maybe needed a little cheering up and maybe a shoulder to cry on. But he still had a premonition, and he lost as little time as possible finding an excuse to be in Molly's neck of the woods. Molly had a sensuality about her that Longarm had felt even when Tom was alive. He'd been ashamed of himself for that. He didn't believe in coveting a friend's wife or woman, but it was hard not to covet, or at least lust after, a woman like Molly. But he had never, to the best of his recollection, ever given her, by sign or word, any idea of how desirable he found her.

It was not that she was all that good-looking, though she was by no means plain. And she wasn't a girl. Longarm figured she would have been at least thirty at the time of Tom's death. Nor did she have a perfect figure. It was just that she had some indefinable something that made men act like they were on the prod the instant they got around her.

Within two weeks after he received the letter he managed to arrange his business so that he was in Wichita Falls at the little house on the outskirts of town where Molly still lived. She received him at the front door with a strange formality, not the hug he normally got. She was wearing a kind of wraparound housedress, the kind with thin material that went around the body once and then was tied with a sash. He could tell, from the way it fit her curves, that she wasn't wearing anything underneath. She got him seated and gave him a drink of whiskey, and then sat across from him, drawing up one leg underneath her. She was barefoot and her hair was brushed and combed, but it fell down around her shoulders. His breath was already coming quicker as he could see her breast clearly outlined in the bosom of her dress, and a glimpse of white, inner thigh as she had her leg tucked up underneath her. She asked, simply and quickly, if he would help her. She said, "It's been over a year since Tom, Custis. A year, and I've respected his memory. But I need a man. Tom would understand. And you were always his best friend. Will you help me?"

Almost in a daze he nodded and finished his drink. She came over, took him by the hand, and led him back to the bedroom. She stood before him as he undressed. Then she asked him to just lie on his back. He did, watching as she untied the sash of her dress and let it fall open. For a second she let it hang from her shoulders, let it frame her beautifully abundant breasts with their big, brown nipples, let it frame her wide, white hips and the little mound of her belly, let it frame her wonderfully shapely legs that seemed to grow out of the brown spreading triangle of hair that began at the V and made a tangled web as it moved up her soft skin. Then she let the dress drop to the floor, moved to the bed, and sat down beside him, staring down gravely at his body. She said softly, "I'd almost forgotten. It's been so long." She reached out with one delicate, soft hand and took his member, already engorged and rigid. Gently she massaged it, moving it back and forth. He gasped with each measure of her touch. She said gently, "Does that feel good? Do you like that?"

He had to gasp, "Careful, Molly. Go slow, sweetheart."

He was so close he couldn't look at her. If he looked at the soft breasts hanging over him, or down at the auburn thatch, he would explode. It felt as if his testicles were drawn so tight against his body they were about to disappear.

She began to kiss him on his body, slowly working her way down. He moaned and writhed, trying to contain himself. Finally he raised up and pulled her to him, burying her mouth in his, kissing her until he could feel her begin to melt. Then he draped her backwards on the bed, threw her legs over his shoulders, and slipped his tongue and his face into the opening, warming, dampening nest between her legs. He could hear her panting, feel her writhing, as he held her balanced by the buttocks in the palms of his hand. She was beginning to cry out as he pulled back and then thrust himself into her, her legs still above his shoulders, now wrapped around his neck. He had brought her so close with his tongue and with his kisses that she climaxed almost at once, thrusting up strongly against him, digging at his back with her fingers, her breath loud in his ear, her breath turning to a low moan. And then, as he exploded, all sound ceased except the pounding in his head. It seemed to go on forever as he'd pumped into her, the pound turning into a *boom, boom, boom, boom, boom.* And then it stopped and he almost slid off her, his eyes closed in exhaustion. She cradled his head in her arms, holding him close and kissing his eyes and his ears and his cheek, whatever she could reach. She said softly, "Wonderful, wonderful. Thank you, thank you."

Gradually their breathing slowed, and then they rested for a time. He slid off her and turned over on his back, his eyes closed. After a time he felt her move, and then felt the gentle touch of her lips and her tongue on his belly. Almost instantly his desire began to quicken. She worked her way down his abdomen very slowly, so slowly that he almost wanted to scream out in agony. Then she took him in her mouth, her tongue working in harmony with her lips. It caused him to gasp and arch his back until nothing but his heels and the top of his head were touching the bed. She continued, working slowly, moistly, bringing him up and up and up. When he thought he could stand it no longer, she slipped away from his member and deftly took one of his testicles into her mouth. She caressed it gently with her tongue and then swiftly moved up, mounting him, straddling him, taking him inside herself. She leaned down to his face. He was panting, gasping. She said lovingly, "Don't wait, honey. Go ahead."

The *boom* seemed just as big, though it didn't last quite as long. After the fires died, she slipped down beside him and held him in her arms for a long time. He contented himself with running his hand up and down her soft skin, sometimes exploring the still-warm, very wet tender flesh that the silken hairs protected. He turned once, and she slipped the nipple of her breast into his mouth and then cuddled him to her. She was so soft, so warm.

Later she got up and, with dark coming fast, cooked them both a steak along with some fried eggs. He slipped on his jeans, not bothering with anything else, and she wore the wraparound housedress with the sash loose. They didn't talk while they ate. When they were finished, he had a few drinks of whiskey while she washed the dishes, and then, without a word being spoken, they went back into the bedroom. They made slow, careful love for a long time. He was as tender and caring as he knew how, working her gently, bringing her up and then letting her ease back down before he brought her up again higher. When he finally entered her and brought her all the way up, she was already trembling and heaving and gasping. Her climax was so strong that the headboard of the bed banged into the wall and broke half loose from the frame. He looked down at her in wonder as she finally lay relaxed, bathed in sweat, her pink mouth half open and gasping for air.

He left her the next morning. His last memory was of her kneeling on the bed naked, putting up her mouth to be kissed and then cupping her breasts in her hands and holding them up for his lips. He was reluctant to leave, both because she would again be alone, and because he would be too. He went back many times, but he was never going to forget that first time.

He asked her to marry him many times, but she always smiled and shook her head no. She said she could never again marry a lawman. "Chances are too good I'd lose you," she said. "I couldn't take it again."

He suddenly came to himself, conscious that a lot of time had passed. He'd been so deep in his memory of Molly that anything could have happened. He glanced up at the moon. It was almost dead overhead, a sure sign that more than an hour or two had passed. He'd been wide awake, staring at the cabin, his eyes occasionally roving over toward the part of the corral that he could see, but he had no memory of anything transpiring during that time. For all he knew, Jack Shaw had made a getaway out the back of the cabin and was five miles away. It was amazing. Longarm had thought of Molly to keep himself awake, and he'd ended up taking a two-hour sleep with his eyes wide open.

He looked carefully from one side of the cabin to the other. Nothing was stirring. Next he looked toward the corral. Besides the packhorse, he could see the whole of one horse and part of another inside the corral. That didn't mean anything. Jack Shaw could have ridden out on one horse, leading another, and left the balance to keep Longarm none the wiser. He glanced back toward the packhorse, trying to see what he was doing. The horse had his head all the way to the ground as if he were grazing, but the only thing around the corral to graze on was sand and rocks. Yet the packhorse kept on as if he had found something to eat. He'd raise his head every few moments and then stand there as if he were chewing. The distance was too far and the light not good enough for Longarm to see if he was or wasn't chewing, but the animal still kept dipping his head down like a horse eating and then raising it back up like a horse chewing. It didn't make a damn bit of sense, but Longarm wasn't going to learn any more by staring into the night. The main problem at hand right then and there was Jack Shaw. Longarm thought of calling out, but it would be just like Shaw to keep still and play possum. Longarm knew that he would do the same if the situation were reversed.

He gazed at the cabin, calculating the distance. It was, he reckoned, about sixty to seventy yards away. A pretty good distance. He took a shell out of his pocket and hefted it. It wasn't quite heavy enough for his purposes, and besides, he needed every shell he had. He put the shell back in his shirt pocket, buttoned the flap, and then began feeling around in the bottom of the wash for rocks or anything he could throw. His hand finally came across a dried clod about the size of his fist or a little smaller. He kept on searching until he'd found another one and a rock about the same size.

As carefully as he could he worked himself around, without raising above the level of the wash, to where he had his legs under him. He peered at the cabin for a long second and then, half rising, drew back his arm and threw the larger of the clods in a high arc toward the cabin roof. To his great surprise he threw it across the angle of the roof so that it landed on the prairie at the left side of the cabin. He hadn't known he could throw so far. With the second clod he stayed more down in the ditch, exposing less of himself. He threw and ducked down, watching as the clod arced across the light sky and landed on the tin roof with a satisfying metallic clatter. The sound of the clod was, very shortly, followed by the sound of three gunshots, the shells making a clatter as they ripped through the tin roof. To Longarm's ear it was a revolver. A handgun made a much shorter report than a rifle. Besides, neither Shaw nor anyone else could fire a rifle that fast.

Well, he thought, at least he knew where Jack Shaw was. He called out, "Sorry to wake you up, Jack. Thought you'd be gone by now."

Shaw sounded angry. "Longarm, you sonofabitch,

53

that wasn't a damn bit funny. Sounded like the damn roof was falling in. I nearly shot myself in the foot getting at my handgun."

"So you was sleeping, was you?"

"Hell, no. I was thinkin' was all."

"Jack, you dozed off. Ain't no crime in admitting the truth."

"I didn't do no such thing. How would you know?"

"Because you fired so fast. You fired like a man was startled awake. If you'd really been awake, you wouldn't have fired at the first sound. You'd of waited to see if it was me or just what. You wouldn't of committed yourself so damn quick."

"Aw, go to hell, Longarm. You ain't so damn smart."

Longarm laughed. His quarry was still at hand. Well, he thought, he'd managed several things in the last little while. He'd killed a pretty good piece of time, he'd startled Jack Shaw, and he'd developed a powerful, powerful longing for Molly Dowd. It had gotten very cool, but he wiped his brow and was surprised to find it was covered with a light sheen of sweat. He resolved not to let himself start thinking again about Molly until he was within at least an hour's travel of Wichita Falls.

Shaw called out. "You ain't so very damn smart, Longarm, as you think. I got way the best of it. I can sleep if I want to because you can't take the chance of exposing yourself to find out if I'm awake or not. Maybe next time you chunk a rock on the roof, I'll do a little possum-playing my own self. I got time on my side, Custis. And don't you forget it. Gonna be dawn in a few hours, and back will come that old sun. I'm fine here in the shade of this cabin. I ain't got to make a break for it. I don't have to take a single chance. The situation will do you in. All you got is a hole wouldn't hide a lizard, a piece of a half-gallon canteen, damn little ammunition, and that sun on your head. Hell, you can't even wear your hat. All I got to do is sit here until your tongue swells up and you go out of your mind with the heat. Then I can go on my way without a care in the

54

world. So don't sound so damn cocky, Longarm. Looks to me like you are the one in the mess."

Longarm thought that that was a fair assessment of the situation. With the exception of the Arizona Rangers. They'd arrive sooner or later. They would come. They couldn't help but follow all of the sign he'd left. Every one of them was a capable tracker in his own right. With him pointing the way they'd make it. The only question was time. He said aloud, "Why can't we figure us out a deal, Jack? Looks like two old friends like us could scheme us a way out of this mess. I got to admit I ain't looking forward to tomorrow. I imagine it will seem like it's forty hours long."

"Of course they's a way out, Custis. You stand up, drop all your firearms, and walk on up here to the cabin. I'll give you a drink of whiskey and something to eat and all the water you want. Got plenty of cool, cool water. That old windmill keeps on spitting it out. Fill your belly with it. I imagine that stuff in your canteen is hotter than my first pistol. Probably tastes of alkali. This here is deep well water. Cool as saloon beer."

Longarm said, "Much obliged, Jack, but I reckon not. Fact is, I been drinking too much water lately. Getting a right bad rust problem according to the doctor."

"Just thought I'd offer."

"One thing I am curious about, Jack," Longarm said, "is how much you got off that robbery. Reason I ask is, I'm wondering if you got enough to maybe retire. The rate you are going through partners, you might have trouble getting a bunch together next time."

Shaw laughed. "Not to worry your old gray head, Custis. I don't reckon I could stand to retire. I'd miss it. I'd miss times like these. Hadn't been for that train robbery, Lord knows when we'd of had this chance to talk. I recollect the last time we visited was down in Mexico, in Durango. You remember that, Custis?"

Longarm smiled grimly. It was an occasion he was not likely to forget. Having a few days off and wanting to sample the wares down south of the Rio Grande, he'd crossed over the border, taken a train, and ended up in the silver-mining town of Durango, which had everything he was looking for in the way of drinking and gambling and women. Every once in a while he liked to get completely loose, and it was a well-honored custom among many federal law officers that they took their business out of the country. The first man he'd run into when he'd walked into a cantina had been Jack Shaw. There had been a dozen warrants out for Shaw, and Longarm had wrestled with his conscience for three days about abducting Shaw illegally and taking him back to the States to stand trial. In the end his legal conscience had won out over his moral and expedient conscience, but he still didn't know if he'd done the right thing. If he'd hauled Shaw back then and there two years ago, there would have been quite a number of people still alive and quite a bit of money still in the possession of its rightful owners. Now Longarm said, "Yeah, I remember, Jack. We butted heads in quite a few hands of poker."

Shaw laughed. "We butted heads on more than that, Longarm. I could see you just itching to board me on a train at the point of a gun and take me back to the nearest border town. I had a bet with two or three hombres that were with me on just that particular score."

"How'd you bet?"

Shaw laughed again. "I bet you wouldn't do it. I bet your conscience wouldn't let you. They thought I was crazy. But I wasn't, was I?"

Longarm said carefully, "How do you know I didn't take note that you had help at hand and know that I couldn't get away with it? How do you know it wasn't that and not conscience?"

"Because I know you, Custis. It ain't your style. If I'd been a foot inside the U.S. border, you'd of tried to take me no matter how much help I had. Or if you'd had any kind of extradition warrant you'd have tried. But you was on leave. Down there to drink and gamble and wench around. I just come as a hell of a big surprise.

And a not-too-welcome one at that. I could see it was troubling you, Custis. Throwed you off your poker game. I believe I won a couple of hundred off you, if I remember correctly.''

"Closer to a hundred," Longarm said. "I was keeping count. I was telling myself I'd have you in a jail someday and I planned to win it back."

"I guess that's what you are thinking about right now, ain't it, Longarm?''

"I'm thinking it is getting damn cold. I got to shut up. Inside of my mouth is near to freezing.''

He didn't know how cold it was, but he reflected that no one was likely to mistake it for a mild night. It always amazed him how the high prairies could go from blazing during summer days to near-freezing at night. All he was wearing was a long-sleeved cotton shirt and denim jeans. He had a jacket and a slicker on his dead horse, but they weren't much good at such a distance. All he could do was hug the dry, rocky dirt and endure, just as he'd endured the blistering sun of the day before. It was part of the job, and would draw high gales of laughter if you put it in your report.

He watched the moon in its slow march across the sky. Soon it would go down, though it set late in such high climes, and then would come a period of darkness that would last a short time until the sun rose. At some times during the summer months, the sun and the moon would almost meet in their ascent and descent. Now and again small cloud masses passed across the sky, making the shadows blink and flutter like the light from a flickering candle.

Sometime later, with dawn not too far away, Longarm became aware of the packhorse again. The horse had backed a little ways from the corral fence and seemed to be having some kind of trouble. Longarm couldn't see him too well because he was in the small shadow cast by the windmill. But he could hear the horse making some kind of gasping and honking noises. If Longarm hadn't known better, he'd have sworn the horse was a mule from the strange noises he was making. As he watched, the horse began to stagger. First he staggered backwards a few yards, and then turned and went sideways. He had his head down, his muzzle almost to the ground. Longarm could see he was very weak in the hind legs, and could not imagine what had come over the horse. He was acting like he was foundering, but all he'd had, so far as Longarm knew, was water, and he'd never seen a horse founder on water. It had been a good twenty hours since the horse had eaten, and there was certainly nothing around the cabin for him to have over-filled himself on.

He heard the horse make the gasping sound again. At the very end it turned into a kind of gurgle. The horse was walking straight toward Longarm, though he was still fifty or sixty yards away. Longarm could tell the horse was in obvious distress of some kind, but he couldn't tell what. He hated to risk a shot in the bad light, but it was hurting him to see the horse in such a condition.

Finally the horse stopped. He raised his head and gasped, and then seemed to turn around and around like a dog chasing his tail. Finally he gave a kind of buck and then a jump. His hind legs collapsed and he fell heavily to the hard ground on his side. Longarm could tell he'd fallen on the side that had been carrying the empty water tin because, in the still, thin air, he could hear the metal grinding as it collapsed under the weight of the horse. The horse made one effort to heave itself back to its feet, then flopped back down. Longarm saw it give one final quiver. After that it lay still.

Longarm stared at the horse. Its head was pointing toward him in his ditch and its tail was toward the corral. The horse lay, Longarm judged, about forty or fifty yards from the west side of the cabin. There was no window on that side of the cabin. He knew that from when he had ridden up. He hadn't seen it, but he doubted there was a window on the east side either. Line cabins wern't built for comfort and windows cost money. A line cabin provided the line rider with a place to sleep and keep his belongings out of the weather. Other than that, the cattleman wanted the rider on about his business of throwing drifting cattle back up to the north. He didn't get paid to sit in the cabin and look out windows.

Longarm lay there, staring at the opportunity. If he could get in behind the horse he would have good cover and a perfect position. From behind the horse he'd be able to see the front of the cabin and all of the corral. Jack Shaw would not be able to even think about chancing a stealthy departure.

But could Longarm make it to the horse and shelter in behind it? He calculated it was a run of close to fifty yards, but there was one advantage. All he had to do was get past the corner of the house. After that Jack Shaw wouldn't have a shot at him unless the outlaw cared to expose himself by leaving the cabin and coming out into the open. Longarm didn't think that Shaw would want to do that. The lawman lay there, staring, thinking.

Chapter 4

It was a risk, but then that was why the Marshals Service paid such good wages. Near as much in a month as he could make in a moderate-stakes game of poker. He glanced toward the cabin. There was just no way of knowing if Jack Shaw was alert and on watch. If Longarm decided to make the move he'd have to take his chances. That was what it came down to. Chances. He calculated the moon would be down in less than an hour, but he doubted that would make much difference. In the twenty yards he'd have to run, in high-heeled boots over sandy, rocky ground, he'd make a shadow against the light sky as clear as a cut-out cardboard silhouette. If Jack Shaw was on watch, the outlaw would have time enough to get off a shot, and Longarm doubted if Jack would miss. The man was a good shot. Longarm had seen evidence of it, and he knew enough to know that a man in Jack's line of work didn't last very long if he couldn't make a shot when he had to.

With his eye Longarm judged the distance over and over, looking for pitfalls in the prairie. It wouldn't be a time for a body to lose his footing or fall. Stumble and fall on that run and a man would be falling for a long time. Might as well fall off the highest mountain.

He looked at the moon again. It was partially covered by some low-hanging clouds just above the horizon. Longarm couldn't tell if it was any darker. Instead, now that the idea of jumping out into the open was in his mind, it seemed to have gotten brighter. He looked back in the direction of the cabin, but there wasn't anything there to see. He glanced at the horse. He was lying very still. Longarm thought that it would be one hell of a bad joke if the horse suddenly got to his feet just as he, Longarm, left the safety of the wash and was about halfway across. Be one hell of a bad joke. He might die laughing from it.

He lay there, cold, glancing back and forth and weighing the risk. Was it worth it? Hell, he couldn't be sure. For all he knew the Arizona Rangers might show up for lunch and he'd have run a hell of a risk for nothing. Or else it might take them three more days to arrive. Could he hold out for three more days? He had water for part of one. And what would he do then? If he got to the commanding position behind the horse, he could make Shaw understand that he was cut off from escape and then he could tell him about the Rangers. It would put a whole new complexion on the matter. Shaw might be willing to strike some kind of deal. Longarm had one in mind, but it wasn't worth a damn unless he could convince Jack Shaw there was no other way out.

The moon was about as low as it was going to get before it went down. Longarm felt around in the dirt until he found the fist-sized rock he'd had before. He got his hat and the canteen strap in his left hand and had his carbine ready to his right. Carefully, slowly, he bunched his legs under him. He'd been lying for so long in one position, he had no idea what kind of spring might be left in his legs. He might jump to his feet and start to run and they'd collapse. Well, he needed a second or two of distraction. All he could do was hope it worked. With his right hand he grasped the rock, and then half crouched and drew back his right arm. He hurled the rock high in the sky, arcing it to land on the roof. The instant the rock left his hand he reached down, grabbed his carbine, and then jumped to his feet, sprang out of the wash, and started running toward the horse.

It felt like he was running in thigh-high mud. His legs were dead. He felt as if he was going nowhere. He had traveled perhaps five or six yards, stumbling and lurching, when he heard the *bang!* of the rock on top of the metal roof. For a second his heart almost stopped at the sound, it had sounded so much like a gunshot. But then his heart got out of his throat and he kept lumbering toward the horse. The horse came nearer. He was ten yards away, and then five, and then two, and then Longarm half stumbled, half dove over the animal's front legs and landed tucked up against the poor creature's belly. It seemed he was hearing a voice in his ears, but his breath was coming so hard and fierce that he couldn't hear.

It was a minute or two before he got himself squared around and facing the cabin. The horse was dead, all right, though as yet Longarm had no idea what had killed him. He laid his rifle over the side of the animal. It was the side that had the load of corn, so it was even higher than just the flanks of the horse would have been. He could hear Jack Shaw shouting.

"Damnit, Longarm! What in hell did you want to go and chunk rocks on top of this damn cabin for? Hell, what business is it of yours if I'm sleeping or not! You got you some goddamn nerve, I'll tell you that. You done made me mad an' I don't like it! Don't do that no more, you sonofabitch, or I'll plow up that ditch of yours with rifle bullets. I got plenty!"

He said, "Settle down, Jack. Hell, I got bored. Had to do something to stay awake."

"What's that?" There was a pause. "Say, where in hell are you? Your voice sounds funny."

Longarm said, "You're hearing things, Jack. Go on back to sleep. I'll chunk another rock about dawn.

Wake you in time for coffee.''

"Say, you sonofabitch, you ain't in that ditch no more! Where in hell are you?"

Longarm looked over at the corral with satisfaction. He could see the whole pen and every horse. He counted five. He could see the barrel, he could see the pipe running out of the windmill, and he could even see a little of the back door. He said, "I don't want to talk no more right now, Jack. This morning air ain't good for my throat."

Dawn just happened. One second the prairie world was a dingy gray, and the next it was as alight as if someone had struck a big match in a room full of mirrors. Just beyond the front of the cabin, Longarm could see the sun crowding its way over the far horizon. It didn't look nearly as big as the golden moon the night before, but Longarm knew it packed a hell of a lot more wallop. While he could he relished the warming rays as they drove the chill out of his bones from the cold night. But he knew it was short-lived comfort. There appeared to be about a solid hour out of the twenty-four when a man could be somewhere near to comfort in this harsh country. One thing about such country, he had often reflected, when you found cheap land you didn't have to wonder what the catch was. It was his personal opinion that they ought to give the damn stuff away to anyone who was fool enough to live on it and try and make a living.

He took a swig out of his canteen for breakfast, and then settled down to be on the alert. There was one large advantage to hunkering in behind the dead packhorse; he didn't have to lay frozen in one position for fear of exposing himself. To get a shot at him, Jack Shaw was going to have to sneak down to one corner or the other of the cabin. If he stayed alert Longarm would have enough of a warning when Shaw tried to sneak a rifle barrel around the corner to take good cover. Now, with the sun up good, Longarm stood up

and stretched and worked his arms and legs back and
forth, trying to get out some of the kinks from the
long, stationary concealment. As he started to get back
down behind the horse he saw what had killed the animal. The big burlap bag that had been on the horse's
right side, full of corn, had somehow gotten ripped
about halfway down. There had been sixty pounds of
corn in the sack, and Longarm estimated that at least a
third of it had spilled out. He glanced over toward the
corral. He could see a jagged crack in one of the
boards of the fence. The horse, in working and strain-
ing his way toward the water barrel, must have
snagged the sack and then ripped it as he'd pulled
away. Looking closely, Longarm could see a little
flattened pile of golden kernels. It was clear that the
horse had filled up on water and then discovered the
corn. He had eaten and drunk all night. The corn, being bone dry, had absorbed the water as fast as the
horse could drink, and had swollen and swollen until
the horse had foundered himself. Just looking, Longarm could see how bloated the horse was. The barrel
of his belly and chest was distended at least two or
three inches. The first time Shaw fired into the animal
he was going to deflate like a full wineskin jabbed
with a knife. Longarm shook his head. It was a hard
way for the animal to die. As well as Longarm under-
stood it, the horse's belly had swollen so much it had
pushed in on its lungs and the animal couldn't breathe.
He wished now that he had risked a shot the night before. Maybe he could have spared the poor animal a
few moments of agony. He sighed. Somebody had
once said that the West was all right for a particular
breed of men, but it was hell on women and horses.

But at least the animal hadn't died in vain. His
death, and the place he'd chosen to fall, had been a
godsend to Longarm. He figured he and Shaw were
now pretty close to being on equal terms. True, Shaw
had the shade and the water and the food, but he
wasn't going anywhere. All Longarm had to do was

find a way to hold out until the Rangers came. A thought came to him. He reached into the burlap bag and came out with a handful of the dried corn. He tentatively tried a grain in his mouth, working at it with his teeth. In a moment he gave it up as a bad job and spat out the kernel. But then another thought came. He unscrewed the cap of his canteen and dropped a dozen of the kernels inside. They'd soak up some of the water, but maybe, with a little soaking, they'd be chewable. He was getting a little tired of desert air for breakfast, lunch, and dinner.

Longarm heard Shaw from the front of the cabin. "Longarm, where in hell are you? Speak up. This ain't a damn bit funny."

Longarm kept quiet.

Shaw's voice got a dangerous tone. "Dammit, Longarm, you better speak up. If you are still curled up in that ditch behind that greasewood, you better either talk or get into a mighty small ball."

Longarm got out the stump of the cigar he'd used the day before and then fished around in his pocket until he'd found a match. He struck it on the thick end of his thumbnail. It flared and he held it to the blackened end of the cigar, puffing hard to get it going through the burnt layer. The cigar was barely three inches long, but he was determined to get all he could out of it. He had damn few comforts left, and he was going to smoke the cigar until it burned his lips.

A shot suddenly rang out. Longarm glanced to his left. He could see a spurt of dirt as a bullet cut through the lip of the wash, cutting through the roots of the greasewood bramble. Another shot rang out, and then another and another, all placed at the base of the greasewood, each cutting a little more off the lip of the wash. Longarm could tell that Shaw was aiming carefully from the precise way the shots were being patterned. It was clear Shaw was cutting down the angle into the wash as much as he could. He wondered if Shaw was back up on his chair, maybe had it leaned against the wall by the door.

Longarm listened patiently and watched as Shaw emptied one magazine in his rifle, then, judging by the lack of time it took, picked up another rifle and kept on shooting. Longarm did not keep count, but he judged that Shaw must have fired somewhere between twenty and thirty shots before he paused. Longarm could see a little furrow cut into the lip of the wash, and could see that a number of the greasewood plants had been cut down at the roots. He felt very glad to be out of the wash. As best he could judge, none of the shots would have hit him, but some would have come closer than the shirt on his back. It would have been an uncomfortable time to be frozen there while Shaw poured in shot after shot. Longarm figured Shaw probably had four or five carbines, or as many as he'd cared to take from his ill-fated comrades.

Shaw said in a loud voice, "That going to make you speak up, Longarm?"

"Hell, Jack, you awake already? Damn, I was just getting breakfast on."

There was a silence, and then Shaw said, "Longarm, you sonofabitch, where are you? You done moved, ain't you? I thought, right after you throwed that rock, you sounded funny. You moved then, didn't you? Only you went to not talkin' so I wouldn't know it while it was still dark, didn't you?"

"You're a hard man to fool, Jack."

"And you let me waste all them cartridges on that damn ditch! Hell!"

"Yeah, but you shot the hell out of that ditch, Jack. If I ever seen a empty ditch get the hell shot out of it, that one did."

There was a pause, and then Shaw said, "Where the hell are you? You're around to the west side of the cabin, ain't you? What the hell you doing around there? They ain't no cover I know of. And you sound too close to be back far enough to be out of rifle shot."

"Maybe I ain't got no cover, Jack. Why don't you step on around and see?"

"What are you up to? I don't much like you around there where I can't get some sight of you."

"That's right, Jack. You never can tell when I'm liable to come crawling up there and snake my way over to that front window and find you sittin' there dumb and happy eatin' canned peaches."

Longarm heard Shaw sigh, then say, "Well, I reckon the game done turned serious, Custis. I reckon it is going to come to a killing."

"It don't have to, Jack."

"Then what are you up to?"

"I wanted to get over here where I could watch the front of the cabin, at least the side of it, but mainly I wanted a good view of the corral and your horses. I never really knew when you might take it into your head to try and break for it, grabbing a horse and taking off south. But now I can. I can see every horse. I can see every foot inside the corral. I can even see a little piece of your back door. You ain't gonna get your hands on one of them horses. Not no way, not no how. At least not alive."

Shaw gave a little bark of brittle laughter. "Hell, Longarm, that's all you know. I could rope me one of them ponies from inside the cabin and bring him in through the back door and have him saddled and ready to go. Come dark I could come out of here at a dead run and be gone before you could get your rifle ready."

Longarm said mildly, "No you couldn't, Jack. You ain't strong enough."

Shaw's voice was puzzled. "Strong enough for what?"

"To drag a dead horse inside your cabin, because he'd be dead before you could tighten the noose around his neck. I can promise you that."

"Don't try and corner me now, Longarm. Don't try and hem me up. I get plumb excited when that happens.

I'm liable to come around one of them corners with a gun going in either hand. I know you ain't got no cover."

"Yeah, I do."

"What'd you do, kill that packhorse? He get tired of drinkin' water and come wanderin' over placed just so?"

Longarm could picture Jack Shaw standing just inside the cabin door, a rifle in his hand, his hand to his ear, trying to place exactly where Longarm was. He said, "Naw, Jack, he foundered himself."

"Foundered himself? On what?"

"I had a load of dried shelled corn on his back, and he ripped the pack and the corn spilled out, and between that and the water he was getting out of your windmill barrel, he managed to do the trick."

"That would just about do it," Shaw said. "I bet he swelled up like an old maid's hopes."

"He'd pop you stuck a pin in him."

"That sun gonna be up pretty good right quick. You reckon he's swelled up now, you let him cure under that sun for a few hours. I reckon by tonight he ain't gonna smell so good. Reckon you can stand that?"

"Well, Jack, I been a lawman a good many years. I reckon I've smelled worse."

"You ain't meanin' nothin' personal by that, be you, Custis?"

"Aw, hell, no, Jack. You ain't lowdown and rotten like some of them crooks I got to deal with. You can't help it because you was born without."

There was a pause. "Without what?"

"Without a conscience. Hell, Jack, you don't know the difference between right and wrong. Punishing you for robbery and murder and various other crimes would be like whipping a schoolboy for liking pie over potatoes."

There was a longer pause. Then Jack Shaw said, "You ain't nowhere near as funny as you think, Longarm. Meanwhile, that sun is going to get higher and higher, and you are going to get hotter and hotter and drier and drier. How much of this do you think you can take?''

Longarm calculated for a moment. Then he made up his mind and said, ''Jack, there is something we need to talk on.''

''What?''

''Well, Hank Jelkco really done you a harm when he didn't cut that telegraph wire. The last thing I did before I left the train and started after you and your bunch was to get off a wire to the commander of the Arizona Rangers company in Phoenix. They could show up today. Or they could show up tomorrow. I figure they can't be more than two days behind me at the most and likely making a hell of a lot better time than I did.''

Shaw said, ''Aw, bullshit, Longarm, you expect me to believe that kind of trifling talk? Hell! Pull my other leg, it's longer.''

Longarm shook his head even though he knew Shaw couldn't see him. ''Naw, naw, Jack. Listen to the sound of my voice. Do I sound like I'm shoveling it up? I tell you there was a wire got off to that headquarters detachment of Arizona Rangers in Phoenix. And I can guarantee you that I marked the trail I was tracking you over. I broke off limbs and I scuffed up the sand. At one point I took a five-dollar shirt out of my saddlebags and tore it into strips to mark the way. They will still have to go through all those jumps and dodges you led me through, but they will get here.''

Shaw was still skeptical. ''Yeah? How come you just now bringing this up? How come you didn't tell me yesterday? How come you waited until you seen you couldn't get me on your own, and figured you'd better invent you some story? Ain't that about the size of it?''

''No, it ain't. I didn't tell you yesterday because you might have taken off on me. I couldn't tell you until I was in this position where I knew for certain I could stop you.''

Shaw had a little worried note in his voice. "You are funnin' me about them damn Arizona boys, ain't you? Them damn Rangers don't like me one little bit. I done made 'em look bad too many times."

"I know that, Jack."

"Hell, they likely to not even take me back into town. They likely to drag me behind a horse, drag all the hide off me. Who would have custody? Hell, you're a federal officer, Custis."

"Yeah, but we are in Arizona Territory and there will be a bunch of them and only one of me. Custody is something you argue about later in court. If a squabble starts over it on the spot, it's generally the strongest side that wins. But I do believe a court would later rule that I, by rights of being a deputy U.S. marshal, would have custody. Or should have had custody."

"Goddammit!" Shaw said bitterly. "That's small comfort, Longarm, damn small comfort. Hell, that bunch is about half outlaws they ownselves. And they is a bunch of Mex's in with them. They liable to skin me alive."

Longarm nodded. "There is that chance, Jack."

There was a troubled silence. Longarm could hear Shaw sigh and curse softly to himself. After a moment he said, "Well, Custis, I appreciate you putting me on to this fact. I reckon now I'll have to take my chances with you. I don't figure you can last. I'm about halfway willing to bet my neck that that sun gets you before it is good and dark tonight. And I'm willing to bet that you might even pass out from that heat. Or go out of your head. What do you reckon?"

Longarm hated to tell him. He was afraid it might make Jack Shaw do something rash. Of course that wouldn't be so bad either. Get this affair over with and get on back to town. Longarm was promising himself as fine a time as a man ever treated himself to if he ever got off this high prairie and back to civilization. He was going to lie in a cold tub of water and drink cold beer and eat one steak right after another. But first he had to give Jack Shaw the bad news. He said, "I'm sorry to tell you this, Jack, but matters ain't going to go in that direction. If I feel I can't hold on until the Rangers get here, I'm going to start shooting your horses, and I'll kill every one of them and leave you in the same shape I'm in. On foot. Out here in the big middle of nowhere. I reckon they'll find you, Jack, no matter what happens to me."

There was silence, and then Jack Shaw said, sounding amazed, "Why, goddamn, Custis, that is just downright mean. Cruel! Shoot a man's horses? Leave him afoot in this kind of country? Don't you know it was for just such reasoning that we started hanging horse thieves?"

"Jack," Longarm said calmly, "I am a lawman. And you did rob a train and kill several of the occupants. We take that kind of serious also."

There was a silence. A little breeze stirred the morning coolness. The windmill blades creaked around, and water poured out of the little pipe and into the water barrel. Longarm looked over at it longingly. It was so close, yet so far away. Even if he was standing at the fence, he didn't have a long enough neck and head like the horse to reach the water that was flooding out of the barrel.

Shaw said, "You shore you wouldn't take some money and let me ride on out, Custis? Hell, I could leave you ten, maybe fifteen thousand dollars American. I'm talking money here, Custis. I know you are square as a preacher's dice, but I ain't worth all this trouble. Hell, you are sufferin' out there, Custis. Whyn't you look the other way for about ten minutes and you'll have you a nice little nest egg to hatch."

Longarm let him talk, waiting for him to run down. When, by the silence, he figured Shaw was through, he said, "Jack, you are starting to run out of time. At least you are gambling with your time. When you are able to see those Rangers coming across the prairie, it will be too late for me to have any control over the situation. You ought to give yourself up now."

"I can't do that, Custis." There was a pause. "I reckon I'm going to have to take my chances on what kind of shot you are. If you last out the day, I reckon sometime tonight I'll mix in with the horses and try and make a getaway for the border."

"You convince me of that and I might have to start shooting horses right now."

"Hell, Custis, you don't understand. I got enough I ain't going to cut up wild no more. I'm heading straight for Mexico and I'm never coming back across that line again. You've seen the last of me. What good will it do you to see me rot in prison or swing at the end of a rope?"

"I'm glad to say I don't have to think 'bout such things, Jack. My orders are just to go out and catch 'em. I don't have to decide if they be guilty or set their punishment."

Shaw said morosely, "I know you ain't bulling about them Arizona Rangers. Bulling never was your style, Custis. Not when it come to serious matters. I hate like hell the situation has come down to this. Hell, Custis, it has got damn serious."

At a little after noon they began talking again. Longarm thought Shaw was starting to weaken enough that he might give serious attention to a proposal Longarm had. He said, "Jack, what kind of wanted paper they got on you in New Mexico Territory? I figure they got some, ain't they?"

Shaw said, the irritation plain in his voice, "You trying to crack a joke, Longarm? Hell, yes, they got wanted paper on me."

"For what?"

Longarm could almost see Shaw shrug. "Oh, little cattle rustling. Robbed a couple of banks. I never done much business there. That's a mighty poor piece of country next to Texas and Arizona. Hell, I figured go where they had the most to steal."

"You ain't got no murder paper out on you?"

"Not that I know of. Let me think. . . . No, no, I don't reckon I killed anybody there. Maybe as a lawman. Hell, it wasn't never my favorite part of the country. Like I say, the damn place is poor an' it's already overrun with all the trash and second-raters you can find."

"And you never killed nobody there?"

"Dammit, didn't I just say so? Hell, Custis, I don't *have* to kill folks everywhere I go. I never killed nobody without it was for profit. What you think I am, some kind of murderin' fool like that idiot they call Billy the Kid? I notice *he* stays around New Mexico. That ought to tell you what I think of the place."

Longarm said slowly, "I got a thought here. It ain't the best you want to do, but it might be the best you *can* do."

"What is it? Hell, I'm open to nearly anything right now."

Longarm hesitated a moment, trying to figure how Jack Shaw would consider the idea. If he was really afraid of the Arizona Rangers—which Longarm thought he had every right to be—then he would have to look favorably at the proposition. Maybe not at first, but in the end he'd have to see it as his best alternative. Longarm wanted him to take it right away because he was already feeling the effects of the sun. He knew his body was dehydrating, and he knew he'd lost too much salt out of his system through sweating. He wasn't certain how long he could hold out. In effect he was going on his sixth day of driving his body to its limit. Even as blessed as he was with a first-rate physical constitution, there was a limit to what he could stand.

Impatiently Shaw said, "Well, dammit, Longarm, you got a idea or not? Speak up, man, don't be bashful."

"All right," Longarm said. "I'll tell you what I'm willing to do. If you will surrender right now. I mean pretty quick. I'm willing to take you into custody and turn you over to territorial law in New Mexico. I don't figure the border is more than forty or fifty miles from here. If I've got it figured right, we ought to have a dead straight shot at Lordsburg, which is just inside the border.''

Shaw said, disappointment in his voice, "Hell, that ain't no idea. That's robbing Peter to pay Paul. Why would I care if you turned me in here or New Mexico?''

Longarm said, "That's why I was asking you what kind of paper they had on you in New Mexico Territory. They'll string you up for sure here. Right away if them Arizona Rangers catch you. And for shore within thirty days even if I get you to federal or territorial law. They ain't gonna like what happened at that train, Jack. I surrender you in New Mexico, you ain't wanted for no hanging offense. You'll go to prison. I ain't going to try and convince you that will be no picnic, because I would imagine you've seen such places when you were a lawman. But at least you'll be alive. And you might escape. It's been done.''

Shaw was silent for a moment. Finally he said, "Aw, hell, Longarm, it ain't no good. I see the point and it is a good one. Yeah, I'd rather a long prison sentence than a short rope. But if you turn me in in New Mexico, the governor of Arizona will write to the governor of New Mexico and back I'll go. They got a name for that. I can't call it to mind.''

"Extradition.''

"Yeah, extradition. I can't see no advantage to that.''

"I'll find a pluperfect ambitious sheriff in New Mexico. He'll fight like a wildcat to keep you, Jack. Hell, you're big political medicine. You got a big name. You got the kind of name they put it in the paper folks will recognize it.''

Shaw got a pleased tone in his voice. "You really reckon?''

"Hell, I know so. Listen, Jack, more than one political career has been built on catching a lot smaller fish than you. I can't see New Mexico letting you go back to Arizona without a fight. And that will take time, time that you are alive, time that you might can figure out a way to make a break, escape. Hell, Jack, anything is better than waiting here for them Rangers to arrive. Crazy as they are. You know what kind of mood they will be in after four or five days of hunting through them crags and gullies for the sign I left. Hell, they might hang *me*.''

Shaw said slowly, ''Weeell, maybe you got a point there, Longarm. Maybe it would be better. Hell, maybe I could escape from you before you delivered me in Lordsburg.''

Longarm said dryly, ''I wouldn't count on that, Jack. I have gone to considerable trouble over you. Wouldn't look too good on my report.''

''What's in this for you, Custis?''

Longarm laughed. ''That's easy. Get in out of this damn sun. Get a good drink of water. Get a meal. Drink some whiskey.''

''That horse startin' to smell?''

''Not yet, but I ain't kidding myself that he won't. But I think them Arizona Rangers will be here before then. You better make up your mind, Jack.''

Longarm could hear Shaw thinking. Finally the bandit said, ''I stay here and the Arizona Rangers will come. Longarm, will you give me your word of honor that they are coming?''

''Why, hell, no, I won't. I can't give you my word of honor on what another man will do. I will give it to you that wires were sent to them and that I left enough sign on the trail that a blind man could damn near follow it, much less that bunch who knows this country a hell of a lot better than you or me.''

''Your word of honor on that?''

''Yes, dammit, I just said so.''

''Damn!'' Shaw said. Longarm could hear him sigh. ''I know what a power you set by your word. I reckon that means they will be coming. The other way is to let you take me to New Mexico. That means a prison where most folks would rather be dead. There is that other choice, though.''

''Trying to make a break out the back? Right under

75

my nose? Hell, Jack, you might as well shoot yourself and save me the cartridges.''

Shaw said thoughtfully, ''I don't know. You been curing out in that sun for quite some time. You right shore your hand will still point and your eye follow? I got to figure you are pretty well wore down.''

Longarm laughed. ''You are talking like a man with a paper asshole, Jack. Hell, at the worst it would be a shot of thirty to fifty yards with a good rifle. I ain't going to miss at that distance.''

''I recollect your rifle was fouled not that long ago.''

Longarm thumbed back the hammer of his rifle and fired a shot into the side of the cabin. Splinters flew from the rock face and the shot boomed loud in the dry, still air. When the echoes had died, Longarm said, ''That sound like it's fouled, Jack?'' He levered another shell into the chamber, listening with his ear close to his rifle for the sound of any grit.

Shaw said, ''Naw, I reckon yore rifle works. Course I ain't so sure about you. You hit the side of the cabin. That don't tell me much.''

''You got a empty whiskey bottle in there?''

''Oh, I reckon I could find one. That or a can of tomatoes.''

''Well, throw one of them out far enough so I can see it from where I'm at.''

A moment passed, and then a clear, empty bottle came flying out of the cabin and landed ten yards short of the ditch, bouncing and rolling. Longarm had it in his sights before it had stopped moving. His shot exploded the bottle into a thousand pieces. He said, ''You satisfied, Jack?''

But just as he was about to lever a shell into the chamber of his rifle he saw, out of the corner of his eye, a rifle come around the back end of the house. He whirled and dropped flat behind his horse as Shaw's rifle boomed and a shot sailed over his head. Without aiming he fired with his rifle resting on the hindquarter of the horse. The slug chipped rock at the exact spot the other

76

rifle had just disappeared from.

It made Longarm angry. He said, "All right, dammit, Shaw. We were negotiating. If that is the way you want to play it, I'm content to let the Rangers have you. And to hell with you!"

"Hell, Longarm, what did you expect? I reckon if you was in this spot I'm in, you'd try anything you could."

"Well, you just run me clean out of patience, Shaw. I'm tired of fooling with you. I've been patient and straight, but all that is over with. You got two chances the way I see it, slim and none. And Slim left town."

Chapter 5

Shaw said, "You plannin' on trussin' me up like a market pig, Custis?"

Longarm laughed without much humor. "Well, I can't take your word if that is what you are getting at, Jack. I reckon you've already made it clear that anything is fair so long as it saves your neck. I'd have to hinder you in some way. I reckon you can understand that. I don't much care for the idea of getting myself killed by trying to do you a favor."

"You figure taking me in is a favor, do you? Didn't you say something about you was getting plenty sick of laying out there in the sun with no water?"

"That's true enough. But I'm willing to do it if you'd rather wait for the Arizona law. But I can tell you, Jack, the minute them little dots appear in the distance, there ain't no more selections. I'll have to turn you over to them."

"You still ain't answered me about binding me up. Custis, I tell you, I can't stand that. It makes me go out of my head. I get to feeling like I can't get my breath. I'd rather be kilt than all bound up."

Longarm said, "Well, I got a set of manacles in my saddlebags. How you feel about them?"

"Wrist cuffs or leg irons?"

"Naw, they are handcuffs, some call 'em. I could fit you out with them. That ought to keep you from being a wide-open threat. You understand, I don't blame you for wanting to get loose. Was I in your shoes and headed where you are, I'd want it too. But Jack, you done the robbing and murdering. Now you got to pay up."

There was a pause, and then Shaw said, "I reckon I could stand the wrist manacles. But would they be in front or back? I ain't sure I could stand to be cuffed with my hands behind me. Minute you stuck my hands behind me, I'd get an itch somewhere in the front or have to blow my nose."

"Oh, I reckon you could keep your hands in front of you. Long as I can satisfy myself you was constrained and couldn't do no harm. You notice I ain't bothering to ask for your word, don't you? Your pledge."

"You done said it once, Longarm. You'd be a damn fool to take it."

"Well?"

"A well is a hole in the ground, Custis. Damnit, don't rush me."

"Turn it sideways," Longarm said, "and it's a mine shaft."

"I reckon you feel like you can make jokes. Well, I don't."

"Jack, that sun is starting to cross overhead. We don't get out of here pretty soon, we won't make enough miles the balance of the day to put much ground between you and them Arizona boys. Now what is it going to be?"

At Longarm's direction Jack Shaw came walking out the front of the cabin until he was plainly in view. Longarm said, "Move on out a little further, Jack, and kind of bend it around toward me. I want to be able to get a good look at you. And you look pretty damn silly with your hands in the air like that. If you've got a weapon on you and you go for it, you ain't fool enough to think I can't pull this trigger and fire faster than you can get it out."

Shaw, walking as he talked, said, "Just trying to get along, Custis. Don't want to spook you into shooting me."

"I ain't got no interest in shooting you unless you make me. Keep that in your heart, Jack, and we won't have no trouble. Now take off your shirt."

Shaw said, "Aw, hell, Longarm. That's just plain silly, tight as this shirt fits. What you reckon I could conceal? That sun could burn the hide off me in ten minutes."

"Take your shirt off, Jack."

Will ill humor Shaw unbuttoned his shirt and then peeled his way out of it. His arms and hands and neck and face were brown and leathery, but the skin covered by his shirt was almost white in comparison with the rest of him. Longarm could see his lean, hard build. The small muscles rolled and rippled as he shucked the shirt.

Longarm said, "Now turn completely around. In a circle."

"Hell, this is getting ridiculous, Custis. Dammit, I've surrendered. What more do you want?"

"You ain't never surrendered, Jack. And you and I both know that. You are only doing my bidding because it is the best for you right now. All right, sit down on the ground, facing me, and take off your boots."

Shaw stood there, his hands at his side, his skin looking whiter under the sun. He said, "I'll be damned if I will."

Longarm laughed silently. By now Shaw was only fifteen yards away from where Longarm was sheltered behind the dead horse. "All right, Jack, don't then. Make a run for the cabin if you'd druther."

"Dammit, Longarm, you give your word!"

"I said I'd turn you in in New Mexico. And I will if you cooperate. Now make up your mind. Either take off your boots or make a run for the cabin. I know what can be hid in a boot because I've done it myself."

Jack Shaw sighed. "Let me save us both some trouble.'' He bent over and started to put his hand inside his boot.

Longarm said quickly and warningly, ''Hold it right there, Jack! Don't you move a hair. I don't know what you think you're doing, but whatever you are reaching for without permission had better be a biscuit or a picture of your girl or something else we can all enjoy.''

From his bent-over position Shaw said disgustedly, ''Hell, it's a gun, Longarm. A revolver.''

''Then you better treat it like a fresh-laid egg. You reach in there with just your thumb and one finger and bring it out and lay it on the ground. I am going to guarantee you, Jack, that it is in your best interests not to startle me or make me nervous.''

''All right, all right.'' While Longarm watched him warily, Shaw drew a large-caliber revolver out of his boot top. He carefully laid it on the ground and straightened up. He said sarcastically, ''There. You happy now?''

''Take five paces backwards, Jack,'' Longarm said evenly, ''and then sit down on the ground and take your boots off.''

''Well, damn it all, if that don't take the cake. Hell, Longarm, what else you want? Hell, it's hot out here.''

''Same deal as before. Take the five steps back, sit down, and take off your boots, or break for the cabin. I'll shoot if you don't do one and I'll shoot if you do the other. Your choice.''

For a moment Shaw looked undecided. Then, grumbling, he sat down awkwardly on a tuft of bunchgrass and slowly pulled off one boot and then the other. He did it carefully, never seeming to let the tops tilt downward. When he was finished he set both boots neatly before him. He said, ''There. You happy?''

''Get up,'' Longarm said. He motioned with the barrel of his rifle, standing up for the first time since Shaw had come out of the cabin. ''Now walk out yonder, north, forty or fifty yards.''

Shaw was already on his feet. He looked amazed, then

angry. "In my damn socks? Hell, Longarm, you crazy? I'll cut my feet to pieces. There's all kind of rocks and whatnot, not to mention bugs and spiders and even snakes."

Longarm motioned with his rifle again. "Watch where you put your feet. You'll be all right. Now go on." He came around the horse and walked toward Shaw, stopping some ten yards short.

Shaw snarled. "Hell, Longarm, you never said nothin' 'bout all this folderol. I thought we was gonna saddle up and get out of here. What's all this about?"

Longarm smiled thinly. "I reckon you can guess, Jack. I don't mind helping you out for old times sake. I just don't want to get killed in the process. Would you do it any different if you was me?"

Shaw turned and started to gingerly pick his way out from the cabin. He was watching carefully where he placed his feet. "Well I damn shore wouldn't treat a friend this way," he said.

"You reckon we are friends, Jack?"

"Well . . . friendly. Hell, I don't know."

"Have you got any friends, Jack? Real friends?"

"Hell, I don't even know what a friend is supposed to be. Yes, I got friends. Ever'body's got friends."

"A friend is somebody you'd do something for even when there was nothing in it for you."

Shaw was about halfway as far as Longarm wanted him. He said over his shoulder, "Then I reckon I ain't got no friends. You got any, Longarm?"

"I think so."

"But I ain't one of 'em, is that it?"

"Ain't known you that long or that often, Jack. Friends ain't that easy to make. Generally you have to get in some kind of test together, see if you both hold up. You don't make friends drinking together or playing cards or whoring around. Them is just acquaintances."

Shaw got out as far as he appeared willing to go. He stopped and turned around. "I reckon then, if I'd been a real friend, you'd of let me go."

"If you'd of been a real friend, I wouldn't have had to let you go because you wouldn't have been in this fix in the first place. And if you had, you'd never have asked me or expected me to turn you loose."

Shaw said, "Aw, bullshit. All yore friends ain't honest."

Longarm walked over to Shaw's boots. He picked up one and turned it upside down and shook it. Nothing came out. He said, "Maybe not, but they damn shore wouldn't do nothing where I had to come for them." He pitched the boot toward Shaw. It landed ten yards short. But the outlaw wasn't watching. He was intent on the second boot as Longarm picked it up and turned it upside down and shook it. Nothing came out, but Longarm didn't look satisfied. He put the boot down on the ground and then knelt by it, keeping one eye on Shaw and shifting his rifle to his right hand. With his left he felt around inside the boot. After a half a moment a soft smile broke out on his face.

Shaw said, "Damn you, Longarm. Damn you to hell!"

Longarm worked his hand hard for a few seconds, and then drew it out of the boot. He had a derringer by the butt end. It had been held inside the boot by a sewn pocket. That had prevented it from falling out when Longarm had upended the boot. But Longarm had noticed the difference in the weight compared with the other boot. He held the derringer up for Shaw to see and said, "Jack, you are a most amazing man. I reckon I better get you to drop your britches. Wouldn't surprise me if you had a rifle tied to one of your legs."

Shaw was furious. "Hell, I had forgot all about it. I wasn't tryin' to slip nothin' past you."

Longarm laughed. "Yeah, forgot all about it. I guarantee you one thing, ain't going to come a time when I forget about a pound and a half of steel in one of my boots."

"You get used to it," Shaw said hotly. "I been carryin' it for years!"

Longarm broke open the action of the little gun, took out the two shells, threw them one way, and then flung the derringer as far to the west as he could.

Shaw said, "That gun cost forty dollars. You plannin' on payin' me for it?"

Longarm picked up the now-empty boot and sailed it toward the outlaw. "Oh, yeah, Jack. You can bet on that. Bet you whole pile on it."

Shaw stood, eyeing him. "Now what am I supposed to do?"

"Go put your boots on and then sit down."

"Where?"

"Right where your boots are."

Shaw was getting angrier by the moment. "Goddammit, Longarm, you are not treating me like a white man. I need my shirt back on. This damn sun is about to peel the hide off me."

Longarm said, "Then the faster you do what I tell you, the faster you can get your shirt back on and get back in the shade."

Longarm could see how fortunate he was in the way his saddle horse had fallen. Probably as a result of being totally played out, when Shaw had shot him, he had crumpled straight down on his own legs rather than falling on his side. He looked, Longarm thought, remarkably like a horse sleeping. But his position was going to make it an awful lot easier for Longarm to get his saddle loose than if the horse had fallen over and pinned a stirrup or was lying on the girth cinch.

But right then all that Longarm wanted was his set of manacles. He stood facing Shaw, covering him with his rifle, while he felt around inside his saddlebags for the handcuffs. His hand almost immediately touched a bottle of the Maryland whiskey, but he resolutely bypassed that and rummaged around until he found the manacles. He pulled them out, starting toward Shaw, only detouring to pick up Shaw's shirt. He came within five yards of the outlaw, who was sitting hunkered down on the hot prairie. Longarm motioned for him to stay down as he came up. He wrapped the manacles in the shirt and pitched the package to Shaw. He said, "Put your shirt on and cuff one of your wrists with the irons. And I better hear it take up to the last click."

It was all done quickly. When Longarm was satisfied, he had Shaw start toward the corral, walking behind him and off to one side. It seemed to Longarm that Shaw was not as tall as he'd remembered. But then, it had been some time since they'd been side by side. Still, he reckoned Shaw to be a least two or three inches shy of his own height of a little over six feet. But that didn't really make much difference. In Longarm's line of work it didn't matter about the size of the man so much as the size of the gun he was carrying. Longarm couldn't remember many instances when he'd had to "scuffle around in the dirt like some schoolboy," as Billy Vail had complained about an arrest he'd made in his earlier days.

At the corral Shaw once again balked when Longarm told him to sit down at the corner post and hug it. "Like your best girlfriend."

Shaw said, "Hell, I know what you want. You plan to manacle me to this post. Well, I won't do it. I want out of this sun."

Longarm said reasonably, "So do I, Jack. But I don't reckon there is anything to hook you to inside the cabin, and anyway, I need to be able to see you. Most of the work is going to take place out here. I don't want you out of sight."

In the end Shaw sat down, put both his arms around the post, and then cuffed his own wrists. Longarm walked over close to see that the cuffs were indeed locked and in place. He said, "Jack, you ought to be proud. I generally don't take nowhere near as much trouble with other folks. But then other folks ain't Jack Shaw. The only person I've ever known was meaner or more dangerous than you was a girl name of Lily Gail

Borden. She was a holy terror. Nearly got me killed a half a dozen times.''

Shaw said, "I don't reckon I care for the comparison." He turned his head and spat. "Some damn woman."

"She wasn't just some woman. She was the original black widow. Don't get it in your mind that you got to be big and strong, Jack. I'm paying you a compliment when I compare you to Lily Gail."

Shaw said, "Hell, Longarm, I don't want to hear none of yore stories. You got me, now let's hurry up and get the hell gone before them Rangers show up."

It took better than an hour to get them ready to travel. Longarm had to get his saddle and bridle off the dead horse and pick one out of the bunch of five he wanted to ride. He asked Shaw which was his horse, and was told it was a big gray gelding who looked strong and powerful and full of go, but he was not the kind of horse Longarm would have picked for the brutal ride. Instead he chose to saddle a lanky, long-legged, lean bay horse for himself that he took to be close to a six-year-old. Shaw said, as if in derision, "That hide was Hank Jelkco's mount. Damn fool."

Longarm didn't know if he was talking about the man's choice in horses or the way he'd forgotten to cut the telegraph wires. As far as Longarm was concerned, an old border cattle thief like Jelkco would have a good idea for a staying horse, a horse with plenty of bottom that could stand rough usage and keep on getting a man down the road. Longarm figured that a man like Jelkco, who wasn't very skillful at anything else, would have to have had a good eye for a getaway horse or else he wouldn't have managed to get as old as he had. His mistake had been not being able to read men, especially men like Jack Shaw. Longarm knew for a fact that many a man was eager to ride with Jack Shaw because he'd been a lawman, which to them meant he'd be straight and fair and know the secret ways to get around the law.

Well, not only wasn't Jack Shaw straight and fair, he didn't know any secret ways around the law, mainly because there weren't any.

Longarm found quite a quantity of revolvers and rifles, along with a good amount of ammunition, inside the cabin. Shaw had a bedroll and several big canvas water bags, but nowhere near as much grub as he'd let on to having. In the end Longarm found a canvas tarp that Shaw had been using as a groundcloth. He turned that into a pack, lacing it over one of the three remaining horses. After that he took time to get himself something to eat. He'd already drunk his fill of water, just standing on his tiptoes, bracing himself against the big, high barrel and sticking his mouth right into the stream of water that was being pumped out of the ground by the creaking, rusty blades of the windmill. Shaw had been right about that part, at least. The water was cool and sweet, almost like artesian water, but Longarm knew that it was a shallow well that had tapped into one of the underground springs that dotted the country. After that he ate some of Shaw's dried beef, a few stale biscuits, and a can of peaches and a can of tomatoes. It was a long way from his idea of a meal, but it beat the hell out of what he had had for the last day or two. He was inside the cabin, enjoying the cool shade, for so long that Shaw started hollering. Longarm just let him shout, and finished off his meal with a good drink of his Maryland whiskey and part of a cigar. He smoked it only a third of the way down, and then carefully tamped it out and put it back in his pocket. He was down to two cigars besides the partial one. That was getting seriously low on tobacco.

When he came out to saddle and bridle Shaw's horse, the outlaw was fairly writhing with fear and rage. He said, "Goddammit, Longarm, are you *tryin'* to get me taken up by them Arizona Rangers? Hell, Grammaw was slow but she was old. What in hell you been doin'?"

"I been having a bite, Jack. Didn't you invite me to?"

"Hell, you can eat up the trail somewheres. We need to get the hell out of here."

"Soothe your mind, Jack. We got plenty of time." Longarm reached in his saddlebags and came out with a short little telescope. He pulled it out to its fullest length and trained it north, toward the last few foothills and mountains where Jack Shaw had come out on the prairie. He looked the country over carefully. All he could see moving was a doe and a couple of fawns. He compressed the spyglass and put it back where it had come from. "So far no sign of them," he said. "We ought to be out of here in about a half an hour. No more. By the way, I didn't see your winnings from that robbery in the cabin. Where are they?"

Shaw looked up at him from where he was sitting on the ground with his hands holding the post. He said, "Why, the money ain't here, Custis. I hid it."

Longarm stopped pulling up the girth on Shaw's gray. He stepped around the horse and shifted his way through two others to get to where he could look directly at the outlaw. "What are you talking about, the money's not here?"

"I mean it's not here."

Longarm stared at Shaw's eyes for a long time. "You are lying, Jack, and there's no sense in it. You ain't going to be able to come back here and claim the money. You are going to prison if you don't catch a rope. Now where is the money?"

Shaw jerked his head toward the north. "I cached it up yonder. Right after I kilt them last two, or kilt the one who kilt the other. I wanted to make sure the coast was clear to the border. I didn't want the money with me. I feared it might give me away." He touched his cheek where the birthmark was. "Not everybody was going to connect me with that robbery like you done."

"Son of a bitch!" Longarm said. He turned and walked away a few steps. "Hell! Hell and damnnation! You have throwed me in a hell of a situation. Damn!"

He stood there staring back at the small mountains, distant in the thin air.

"What the hell is the matter?" Shaw said. "What are you so riled up about?"

Longarm faced around to him. "Hell, Jack, think for a minute. I bring you in in New Mexico. And I bring you in without the money. It ain't going to look good. It ain't going to look good at all. Not even a little bit."

Shaw said, "Aw, hell, Longarm, ain't nobody gonna suspect you of stealin' that swag. Hell, they'd suspect the President first."

Longarm went close to him. "Are you lying to me, Jack?"

"Hell, no. I swear I stashed that money back just at the foot of the mountains. And for the reason I give you."

Longarm glanced at the far-away hills. "I ain't sure I believe you. How much was the take?"

Shaw looked hesitant.

Longarm said, "Dammit, Shaw, I ain't putting up with this. Now, how much was it?"

Shaw grimaced. "Little over sixty thousand, though I didn't count it down to the last ten spot."

"How'd it come?"

"Some paper money, but mostly gold coin. Eagles and double eagles and twenty-dollar gold pieces. Some fifty-dollar gold cartwheels."

"Sixty thousand, huh?" He whistled. "Not bad, Jack. No wonder you didn't want to share."

"It's what I meant about not ever comin' back here again. I figured to live the rest of my life on that money in Mexico."

Longarm said with disgust, "Aw, hell, Shaw. You couldn't have gone six months without getting up to some crookedness. Do you really think you rob and kill for the money?" He suddenly shook his head. "The hell with that. You say you ain't got it here?"

Shaw shook his head. "I'm telling you, Custis. It's back yonder. A good fifteen, twenty-mile ride."

Longarm said, "We'll see." He went through the back door and into the dim interior of the small cabin. He looked slowly around, up and down the walls and at the ceiling. The floor was hardpacked dirt. He walked carefully over it, looking for any signs of disturbance. There were none. Neither could he find a shovel or any other digging tool. The only tool about the place was a wooden-tined pitchfork, and he couldn't see where much could be done with that.

He walked slowly around the perimeter of the room, looking for places in the rock where something might be secreted. But sixty thousand dollars in coin and paper was quite a little bundle to hide.

He looked toward the ceiling, toward the few rafters that stretched across the roof. There was no sign of anything or any sign that anything had been disturbed. There was a small fireplace with a rock chimney. The fireplace was empty, but Longarm got down on his hands and knees and looked up the chimney. All he saw was a square of light blue sky.

He went back outside through the front door and walked carefully around the cabin and the corral, looking for any sign of where the money could be hidden. There was nothing outside on the featureless plain and nothing he could see inside the corral that might do for a place to make a cache. Shaw was swearing and cussing with every step Longarm took. "Dammit, Longarm, we got to get out of here! You gonna git me hung. Hell, I give myself up to you to avoid that. Now you goin' to stick around here until it be too late. If I'd of stayed in the cabin I'd of at least been able to make a fight out of it. Damn you, Longarm, the goddamn money is not here!"

Longarm didn't bother to answer. He stood, staring. It could be on the roof, but he didn't see a ladder or any way of climbing the sheer walls of the cabin. Still, it might have been thrown up there with the idea of coming back with some way to get up there. He could at least have a look.

He ducked through the corral fence, went over to the windmill, and began carefully mounting the rickety iron rungs of the ladder that ran up one of the legs of the water-drawing apparatus. On the ground Shaw continued to cuss and rant. It only took Longarm about four rungs to be able to see on top of the cabin. Except for a few pieces of tumbleweed, the metal roof was bare. He came thoughtfully back to the ground.

Shaw said urgently, "You gonna get me hung, Longarm."

Longarm looked north toward the hills. He said, "You say it is cached back yonder?"

"Yes, hell, yes! Ain't that what I been saying?"

Longarm sighed. "Then I reckon we will have to go and get it."

Shaw went almost pale under his tan. He said, choking on the words, "Are you plumb loco? We'll ride straight into them Arizona Rangers! They'll stretch my neck like India rubber."

Longarm looked at him. He said calmly, "Yeah, that's probably what will happen."

Shaw swallowed visibly, his Adam's apple bobbing up and down in his lean neck. He said, his voice weak, "Longarm, you can't do this to me. Hell, you are not that sort of man. Hell, you gave me your damn word of honor!"

Longarm was watching him closely. He could see fear in Shaw's face and eyes. He didn't think he'd ever seen the man afraid before. In fact he had a reputation for being fearless. Longarm shook his head. "You got it wrong, Shaw. I give you my word of honor that the Arizona Rangers had been telegraphed. I didn't give you my word of honor about nothing else."

Shaw said, "Dammit, Longarm. I am in your custody. I'm your prisoner. You got to look out for me."

Longarm said, "And you claim that money is hid in the first part back there of those hills."

"Hell, yes! Listen, I can draw you a map. As you come out of the last of the bigger hills, the path leads

91

you down a wide little draw with some of that big Spanish dagger cactus all around. Off to the side is a jumble of big rocks. It was the perfect place for a hidey-hole. You wouldn't never expect to find nothin' in there except tarantulas and rattlesnakes. Hell, I swear it is there, Longarm. You can take me into New Mexico and turn me in and then head back for the stash. I give you my word you won't have no trouble.''

Longarm stood, thinking. He hadn't felt altogether right about taking Shaw over the line into New Mexico Territory. Now this, this about the money. He wasn't sure. He'd been willing to transport him, not so much to keep him out of the Arizona Rangers' hands, as to take him into custody before it was too late. He knew he himself had started to fade, and he wasn't sure how much longer he could have held out. It was a trade, and one he wasn't too proud of, but hell, it all came down to the same thing. Shaw would get sent to the territorial prison in Alamogordo, and not a hell of a lot of men walked out of such places. And there'd be some in there who would recognize Jack Shaw as the lawman who'd sent them up. Longarm wasn't too sure but what, after a few months of that, Shaw wouldn't prefer a quick hanging.

Shaw said, "Custis . . ."

Longarm looked at him. "What?"

"I give myself up to you on the understanding you'd surrender me in New Mexico Territory. You can talk it all around any way you want to, but it comes down to the fact that you made me a deal. Maybe you didn't give your word on that particular part of the business, but we had us an understanding.''

Longarm sighed and looked away. Shaw was right. He had, in effect, entered into a deal with the man. And that deal was, as Shaw had said, to surrender him in New Mexico. If they went back to the mountains, they would run into the Arizona Rangers just as sure as it was going to get hotter. And if they ran into the Rangers, he would have a hell of a time maintaining custody of

Shaw. They'd want him and they'd want him bad, and there would be more of them than there were shells in Longarm's revolver, even if he was willing to make a fight out of it. They'd be on the prod and they'd act fast and figure to argue it out later at their leisure.

He looked at Shaw. "You are putting me in a hell of a position. But you are right. You did surrender to me on a certain condition." He reached into his pocket and took out the key to the manacles. "I'm going to pitch this over to you. You unlock one wrist lock and then pitch me the key back. After that you can see to putting lead ropes on them three ponies we won't be riding. Then handcuff yourself again. I reckon I better see to getting some water."

"I can do that," Shaw said hurriedly. "I can see to getting the water. I can see to it all. You just set down with yore rifle where you can keep a bead on me. I am much obliged, Custis. I really am. I'll get us ready before you can skin a snake. You won't regret it. I promise."

Longarm gave him a sour look. "Then how come I don't feel better?"

"Just the lawman side of you worrying," Shaw said. "That's all. I need to step into the cabin and get them canvas water bags and fill them up while that windmill is turnin' and that little stream of water is flowin'."

"Go ahead." Longarm stood by the side of the back door, his rifle handy in his hands. "If we're going we better get going."

Chapter 6

They had been riding for perhaps an hour, heading a little north of due east. Longarm had the three extra horses, one of which was carrying the pack, on long lead ropes that were tied to Jack Shaw's saddlehorn. If he tried to break for it, he'd be encumbered until he could untie all three ropes, and Longarm didn't think he could do that. Longarm had Shaw's hands manacled together, but they were in front of his body and the cuffs had a foot of chain between them. Longarm rode to Shaw's left and slightly behind.

Several times Longarm had looked back, toward the low line of hills that led to the mountains. Now, on top of a small rise in the prairie, he called a halt and looked back again, his eyes searching the far-distant elevated terrain. Finally he turned in the saddle, reached into his near saddlebag, and came out with his spyglass. He extended it and put it to his eye, concentrating on a small area of the foothills. The ten-power telescope instantly brought the view closer. What he had thought were little ants suddenly turned into mounted men winding their way down from the hills and striking the high plains. He guessed there were at least a dozen, maybe more. Without a word he leaned out of the saddle and handed the telescope to Shaw.

It took Shaw a moment to locate the area, but Longarm could tell when he did by the sudden jump he gave. Shaw said, "Hot damn! That's them and no mistake!"

Longarm reached out and took the telescope out of Shaw's hand. He collapsed it and put it back in his saddlebag. He said, "Let's move on, but we better move slow. This ain't a good time to be raising a power of dust."

They had gone a half a mile before Shaw spoke. "You weren't lying, Custis. I'm obliged to you."

"I don't generally lie about serious matters. This ain't exactly a poker game or a courting excursion. But you don't have no reason to feel obliged to me. The fact of the business is, Shaw, that I wasn't sure how much longer I was going to be able to hold out. I come out of them mountains and hills pretty well wore out and low on water. And that sun was cooking me. I was going to be well done in a mighty short time. So you could say I'm doing what I'm doing for the law and for the lawman."

Shaw said, "Yes, I reckon that is true. And I took that into account. But you offered me the deal when you was taking the sun under a dead horse. You kept your word once you had me in irons. You didn't have to do that. You could have staked me out to a corral post and sat in the cool of the cabin and waited for the Rangers to come. You didn't have to keep your word."

Longarm said, "I don't know what you are talking about."

Shaw gave him a faint smile. "I know you don't. I can't think of another man I'd of trusted in that situation. But I knew you'd stick to the bargain."

"Jack, you talk a hell of a lot. You know that? You don't have to say everything you know like some damn woman."

Shaw said, "I thought you was gonna stick there for a moment on the loot."

Longarm grimaced. "Don't remind me. Dammit, I am going to look bad about this."

Shaw laughed. "You haven't got a thing to worry about, Custis. I'm going to give you all the details about that cache that you need."

Longarm shrugged philosophically. "Well, Jack, if you're playing me false, there is nothing I can do about it. But that money isn't going to do you a damn bit of good. I know you figure to break out of jail or prison or wherever and go back and get that money, but I don't think that is going to be the way the stick floats."

The sun was burning hotter than ever, it seemed to Longarm. He had soaked his hat and shirt and bandanna under the water, getting them as wet as he deemed possible. They had felt like the cool touch of a virgin when he'd put them on, but they'd dried out in half an hour and now there was no relief. He was heading toward where he hoped would be another line cabin, about fifteen miles distant from the other one. It was no certainty, however, as the cabin they'd used might have been the last in the line.

But Longarm desperately wanted to find some shelter and more water for the horses. He and Shaw had ample water with the water bags, but they were a long way from any natural water. Longarm could only hope that there would be another line cabin, that they would find it in the trackless wastes, and that it would have a working water well.

As they trailed over the plains, it was clear that they were on a part of the range that was closed until the autumn. There wasn't a cow in sight. In fact, except for a jackrabbit now and again, or a skulking coyote, there was nothing else alive that Longarm could see.

Shaw had not wanted to make for the line cabin. He'd feared that the Rangers would pick up their trail at the first cabin and run them down. Longarm had assured him that the Rangers couldn't possibly reach the first cabin before dark and they'd be in no mood to trail anyone anywhere. He'd said, "They'll be as give-out as I was, and their horses about the same. All they'll want to do is get everybody well watered and then get some grub and cover their backs with their bellies and have a rest.''

Shaw had argued that fifteen miles wasn't much of a lead. Longarm had said, "They can't go no faster than we can. You want to duck south? That's exactly what they'd figure you to do and that's where they'll go to cutting for sign. Besides, as chewed up as this country is, it is damn hard to pick up and cut out any one set of tracks. By tomorrow morning our tracks will be blowed over likely as not. All they are going to figure is that you are cutting for the border and they will concentrate on that.''

Shaw had said, "Yeah, but what happens when they see you ain't leavin' no telltales like you had been?''

Longarm had smiled. "They'll reckon you done me in. But one thing we got to get straight, Jack. We ain't partners and the decisions ain't open to argument. Your job is not to fall off your horse and not to irritate me no more than is absolutely necessary. Other than that, you are along for the ride.''

They had gotten away, by Longarm's watch, which he thought was still telling the correct time, at three o'clock. Sundown, he reckoned, would come around seven o'clock. If the line shack was no more than fifteen miles away, they should make that with time to spare and without pushing the horses. Before they had left he'd worked the grain sack loose from the dead pack-horse and spread the corn around for the five horses. It wasn't much, but it was better than the dead bunchgrass that was all there was else for them to eat. But it wasn't feed he worried about for the horses. It was water. Lack of feed would only make them skinny; lack of water would kill them.

They had been riding about three hours when Jack Shaw said, "Longarm, how come you don't hate my guts?''

It surprised Longarm. It was not something he'd given much thought to, not in the case of Jack Shaw or most of the outlaws he dealt with. He said, "I don't know what you mean, Jack. Why should I hate your guts?''

''Well, for openers I've pulled every dirty trick on you I could think of, all the way from talkin' you into lighting up so I could get a shot at you to concealing two guns in my boots.''

Longarm laughed. ''Hell, Jack, that's your job. I would have been surprised if you hadn't pulled something. Hell, you're a bandit, an outlaw, a robber. I ain't ever likely to take you for no circuit preacher. But one little item, you didn't exactly fool me with that cigar business. I had my own plans for that.''

Shaw nodded. ''Yeah, that one kind of misfired on me. Or at least your rifle did. Yeah, you really suckered me on that one. I wasn't near as smart as I thought I was. Naw, what I reckon I mean is I'm just about as opposite of you as you can get. I ain't got no notions 'bout myself being anything other than what I am. But a man like you ought to despise me. I would if I was you.''

Longarm shook his head. ''Ain't no profit in it, Jack. You're like you are because, well, just because you are. I do my job by not letting you do yours. Or at least not letting you get away with it.'' He suddenly paused and laughed. ''When you think about it, Jack, I'm kind of beholden to you. If it wasn't for you and your kind I'd be out of a job.''

Shaw swung his head around, frowning. ''That's a hell of a thing to say. What do you mean, me and my kind? Ain't nobody like me. Hell, don't be lumpin' me in there with the rest of that trash don't know how to eat with a fork or when to spit and when to holler and can't read nor write even their own names. I come from a good family and I had eight years' schoolin'. I was even married once.''

''I'm sorry, Jack,'' Longarm said. ''I didn't know you was touchy on the situation. I also didn't know you'd ever been married. What happened?''

Now it was Shaw's turn to laugh. ''Damnedest thing. I married her whilst I was the high sheriff in Brownsville. Only white woman in the county, I think. Things was a little wild back then. That devil Cortina, the one that called himself the Red Bandito, was cutting up pretty good and trying to steal everything that wasn't tied down. She quit me and went back up to Houston. Said I was in too dangerous a line of work."

Longarm smiled. "If she could see you now. Only about ten miles from a party of Rangers every one of whom has a rope and the urge to use it."

Shaw looked annoyed. "That ain't a damn bit funny, Custis."

"Aw, take it easy, Jack. You're well away from them."

They rode a little further, and Jack Shaw said, "Naw, I mainly meant you ought to hate my guts because I used to be a lawman, like yourself, and I turned. I meant that as the reason. Like you might see me as a traitor."

Longarm said lightly, "First off, Jack, you ain't never been and never was gonna be a lawman like me. Like yourself, they is some comparisons I don't care for. If you'd been a lawman like me you still would be one. *Saavy?*"

Shaw glanced back, his lip curling a little. "Yeah, if that's the way you'll have it. Ain't no matter to me. Though I reckon I ain't the first has swapped sides of the badge."

"Lord, no!" Longarm said. "When I first come out here as a deputy U.S. marshal, it was about as catch-as-catch-can an outfit as you ever saw. We all worked for a federal judge. I was under one out of Fort Smith, Arkansas, and worked the Oklahoma Territory. Hell, you never knew from one day to the next whether you was gonna be drinkin' whiskey with your fellow marshals or looking to hang them. I tell you them was some uncertain times. And I wasn't much more than a young sprat hardly dry behind the ears. Was plenty of chances to take a wrong turning in the road."

"And you was never tempted?"

Longarm let out a hoot of laughter. "Naw, Jack. Hell,

no. I loved that low pay and hard work and times. You even had to buy your own cartridges back then. Made a man a better shot, I'll tell you that. Though I don't reckon that was the intention. Tempted? Well, you show me a happily married man that don't take a peek at a pretty woman from time to time and have little thoughts pass through his mind, and I'll show you a man has never been tempted. I ain't got no wings, Jack. They ain't standard issue.''

Shaw said, ''Well, it seemed like you never passed no judgment on me. Even that time down in Mexico when we shared some whiskey and women. You never said nothing. Never asked me nothing.''

Longarm shrugged. ''Man does what he wants if he can get by with it. I don't judge 'em, I just catch them as wants to do what's against the law. I've executed a few, but that was their choice. They had the selection of giving themselves up.''

Shaw looked back at him curiously. ''Well, that's being their judge. Ain't it?''

Longarm shook his head. ''Naw. They judged themselves. Any man that charges straight into certain death has done called the turn on himself and goes out to get what he deserves. I was just the executioner in the business. They was the ones put themselves on the gallows.''

''You really believe that? You really believe a man will sentence himself to death?''

Longarm nodded. ''I do.''

''Why? Why should they?''

''Either out of remorse or conscience or embarrassment or not wanting to stand trial. Some that I had caught had had a taste of prison and knew they couldn't take no more. Though I hadn't ought to be talking about that last to you, considering where you are headed.''

Shaw said, ''I ain't worried about prison.''

''You figure you can handle it? What happens if you run across some of them you put the catch on?''

Shaw shrugged. ''I'll worry about it when I get to it. I'm still trying to figure out what you said about somebody running into a bullet because he done something wrong. Remorse? Was that the word you used?''

''Yeah. I wouldn't worry my head, Jack. I don't reckon there's any chance of something like that coming all over you and causing you to lose your head.''

''You don't think I know right from wrong, do you?''

''I know you know right from wrong. I just think you don't care.''

''Would you be interested in knowing what caused me to hit the owlhoot trail? To turn the badge around?''

Longarm wasn't particularly interested in knowing, but anything that would take his mind off the heat would be welcome. He said, ''If you're a mind to speak about it.''

Shaw pulled up his horse and unhooked a canvas water bag from his saddlehorn. Longarm rode up to him, but kept his distance. The trailing horses were content to hang back, their heads drooping, their tails switching idly in the heat. Shaw unscrewed the cap of the water bag, got the opening up to his mouth, and then lifted the bag until the water gushed into his mouth and then overflowed as he poured faster than he could drink. He lowered the bag and said, ''Ah! Damn, there's plenty of times water is better than whiskey.''

''You better be a sight more careful with that,'' Longarm said. ''I ain't all that sure we'll find water tonight.''

Shaw hung the bag back on his saddlehorn. He made no move to kick his horse on forward. He said, wiping one sleeve across his face, ''I wanted to see what it felt like to be bad.''

Longarm stared at him a moment trying to see if he had heard right or if Shaw was serious. ''What?''

Shaw spat over the side of his horse. The heart-shaped birthmark was not as distinct in the tangle of his unshaven whiskers. They were black and gnarly, as was his hair. He said, ''Ever since I could remember, my ol' daddy had beat goodness in me. I done the least little thing, it was out with a switch or his razor strop or whatever. When I got older, it was a pretty fair-sized paddle. My ol' daddy set a pretty good amount of store by being good. So did my ol' mama, though she generally left the lickin' to my ol' pa. I grew up believin' that if you done bad or wrong you got a lickin'. A hard lickin'. A real hard lickin'. I didn't know much about being good. I wasn't taught to be good, I was taught not to be bad. I never knowed there was a difference. Anyway, that day I was in the bank in Del Rio, I didn't go in there to rob it.''

"You didn't?''

Shaw shook his head. "Naw. I never made no plan, didn't have no more plan than a fly in a jelly jar. I was standing there, in that bank, and they was starting to bring all the money out of the safe and put it in the tellers' cages. All of a sudden I wondered what would happen if I just up and took that money. I knew if you took cookies or pies or whatnot out of the kitchen you'd get a lickin'. But I didn't know about taking money out of a bank. So I just up and drawed my gun, me the town marshal, and took the money.''

"Just like that?''

Shaw nodded, his face serious. "Just like that. Just robbed and ran. Never planned it more than a second before I drawed my gun. I about halfway expected my ol' pa to come round the corner with a good-sized stick and go to flailing away at me. But he didn't.'' Shaw spat again. "So that's how I come to rob my first bank, because I wanted to see how it felt to be bad. Know what?''

"What?''

Shaw grinned. "I liked it.''

"You liked it?''

"Yeah. I liked it a lot. Made me feel good. I kept waiting for that lick from the paddle to land and it never did. Fact of the business is, *I* was handing out the licks, so to speak.''

"And you didn't plan it, that first robbery when you got away with so damn much money? Just a kind of spur-of-the-moment affair, you say?"

Shaw laughed. "Spur-of-the-moment, hell. Spur-of-the-instant more like it. One instant there is all that money coming out because the bank is opening, and the next instant I got my pistol out and am taking that money."

"Didn't have no getaway planned?"

"Getaway? Hell, I'd hard-tied my horse so that I nearly couldn't get the knot out of the reins. It was on account of that I had to shoot the first feller coming out the door." He grinned. "He took the lickin'. Not me."

Longarm started his horse forward. Shaw did likewise. One of the trailing horses came up abreast of Shaw's horse on the left side, working in between him and Longarm's animal.

"And that is how you come to turn in your badge? All them years of robbing and shooting come from a curiosity you had."

Shaw nodded. "Yep. I'd have to say that was true."

Longarm shook his head slowly. "Well, I guess that explains it a little better."

"What? Explains what?"

"Oh, the way you are. The way you ain't got no hesitation about plugging anybody, whether they be your partners or not. I always wondered about you. I always kind of thought you was about as cold-blooded as any hard case I ever run across. I reckon that any man that can turn from town marshal into bank robber just to see what it feels like don't give anything much thought."

Shaw said, "I don't know I much like the sound of that. You give some thought to how long I been operating and how few times I been caught. That ought to make it clear that I give plenty of thought and planning to every caper I pull off. I knew that first time was blind luck. It still scares me sometimes when I think about it. That's why I'm so careful now. You asked me about why I stayed in them mountains so long, jumping from one little range over into another. Well, it's that kind of thinkin' has made me successful."

Longarm looked at him carefully. "I didn't mean that kind of thought, Jack. I meant thought about what you were doing and the rightness or wrongness of the matter, the consequences."

Shaw laughed. "Oh, I get it. Like what you was talking about them folks had run judgment on themselves and stepped into a situation where you had to kill 'em. Well, no, I don't speculate on them kind of matters for one second. I'll never let you be my executioner because I feel guilty, Custis."

Longarm smiled. "You done proved that. Now we better get along. It's getting late and we ain't spotted that cabin yet."

Shaw said, "Damn, I am nearly dying for a woman. How about you, Custis? Could you stand a little?"

Longarm's thoughts immediately flew to the image of Molly Dowd. He said quickly, "Dammit, don't start talking like that with us out in the middle of the desert. Just save that talk for another time."

"You going to let me get to a woman before you turn me in, Custis?"

"Dammit, shut up, I said. I been out in this country as long as you have. So save that talk until it will do some good."

Shaw laughed. "Aw, hell, Longarm, I'm serious. Who is the best woman you ever knowed?"

"My mother," Longarm said shortly. "Now shut the hell up."

"Now Custis, they has got to be one woman that has stood out for you over the years. I know I've had two I ain't ever going to forget."

"Well, do us both a favor and forget 'em for the time being."

"Just tell me if you generally favor darker women— you know, Mexican and such—or do you like 'em light-skinned and blond?"

Longarm rode his horse a little out to the left. "Mostly I like them handy if there is any of this kind of talking to be done. Do you take my point?"

"Well, what was the best you ever had? Can you remember that? I mean, I've had a piece off a woman was the best I thought it could get. Then I've gone back to that same woman and it wasn't shucks. How do you explain that?"

Longarm was silent, refusing to be drawn into the debate.

Shaw sighed. "Seems like at times like this the best you ever had was the last one. That's what I feel right now. I wish to hell I was in bed with them two Mexican women of mine right now."

Longarm was forced to speak. He could not help himself. "You take 'em on two at a time?"

"Well, sometimes. You want to hear about it?"

"No," Longarm said firmly. "It ain't good manners to talk about women. Now shut your trap. We got to make some miles."

Chapter 7

He wished to hell Jack Shaw had kept his mouth shut about women. The minute he'd mentioned the subject, Molly Dowd had jumped into Longarm's mind, and in trying to force her out of his senses Lily Gail had somehow horned in, and you couldn't get Lily Gail out of your mind, not that easily, not without something else to think about besides the blank prairie and the blazing sun that left you about half light-headed, and not if you'd been without as long as Longarm had.

Lily Gail. She'd had several last names in the short time Longarm had known her. She was always claiming to have just been married, which was why her last name had changed, but her husbands seemed to have recently gotten killed. One of the reasons for that was that she seemed to pick her husbands out of the Gallagher gang, which had terrorized Oklahoma Territory and eastern Arkansas for a good ten years. Longarm had first met Lily Gail when she'd been used as bait to lure him into a trap, and a well-baited trap it was.

Lily Gail was a smallish woman in her mid-twenties, though there was still a lot of the girl about her. She had golden, butter-colored hair that she wore just to her shoulders, usually with a little bow up front. The surprising thing about her hair was that her pubic thatch was just as golden, but it seemed to have an interweaving of strawberry color running through it. Longarm had studied that silken little patch at very close quarters. It grew out of the notch where her white and, oh, so smooth inner thighs met, spreading upward and outward to form an arrowhead as if it were pointing the direction to where the treasure lay, which it was. Then, with her legs up, you could see as the little threads of fuzzy silk ran down and around her vagina on both sides, sort of framing what lay between. It seemed as if the careless little hairs grew more golden red as they came closer to that little pink nest that they were protecting. All Longarm knew was that it made the most exciting maze of colors when you took both of your thumbs and opened up her vagina, seeing it go all pink and seeing the inner lips rise and come toward you, already glistening with moisture and seeming to have an inner pulse that you could feel as you lowered your lips to meet them.

Lily Gail had a vagina like none he'd ever found on any other woman. She could seem to open it so you almost felt you could get your head inside. But then she could constrict it so that she could close down on your member and rhythmically milk it and massage it while you wanted to go out of your mind with a pleasure that was so intense it was almost painful.

For a small girl she had surprisingly big breasts. But they didn't droop. Instead they stood firm and erect, her nipples big as cherries almost pointing upward. She liked those sucked. She liked to hold your head in her hands and move you back and forth from one to the other, all the time moaning and jerking her hips. Then she liked to take your head and move you down her stomach, down through the forest of golden hair that carpeted the fat, little mound at the bottom of her belly, down through that to where she could suddenly drop your head with her hands and, so quick it seemed they'd already been there, swing her little legs up and catch you in a grip and hold you there. Then she would thrust at your mouth and tongue, thrust and writhe and gasp and pull at your hair.

Longarm never talked about his women. And he knew that, even if he did, he could never talk about Lily Gail because he didn't have the words to describe her. He didn't know how to say, "She never gets enough," with sufficient impact so his listener would understand that he was saying, "I mean, SHE *NEVER* GETS ENOUGH!" So he had never tried. He had simply run Lily Gail through his mind in slow sequences the way you sometimes saw things so clearly and so easily in a gunfight. The other man is reaching for his gun and you can see it, almost to where the blue is worn off around the cylinders, can see it as he has the gun half out of the holster, can see it as the revolver keeps on being drawn. But you are not worried because you know that you are still comfortably ahead of the man, know that you have already cleared leather and are starting to bring your gun up while he is not yet clear. You can see him now starting up, but you know he is too late. You almost feel sorry for the man, do in fact have the time to feel sorry for him, for your arm is already out and you are pointing where you are looking and squeezing the trigger and dust is suddenly popping our of his shirt where the bullet has hit and the man is going backwards even as he is still trying to bring his revolver up.

Longarm could see Lily Gail like that, but he couldn't describe it. He couldn't describe her mouth, for instance, which was constantly kissing or sucking or licking. Once she got close enough, she fastened onto you with that mouth, perhaps onto your own mouth, and after that she had some part of you in it, even if it was just a finger or your knee, whatever she could reach.

She seemed to almost melt into you, seeming somehow to get inside you and at the same time wrap herself around you. She had a thin little layer of what Longarm thought of as baby fat, and maybe that was what made her feel so soft and pliable, so *enterable*. He could remember the first time, when he'd been chained to a post in the barn, waiting for the Gallaghers to come and kill him, and she'd come out in the late night and, by lantern light, had teased him as she'd taken off her clothes. Then she'd gotten on her hands and knees and backed toward him, with that beautiful round moon of what seemed like a single buttock except it was slashed with the pink ribbon through the middle. She had backed up to him as he'd waited on his knees, with orders not to move his hands off his head, and she had somehow, without his hands or hers as guides, reached up and pulled him into her, and then kept backing and backing until he could not believe he was so deep inside her, and still she kept backing until he almost felt like *she* was inside *him*.

Then, without using her hips or allowing him to move, she had worked him and worked him with just that muscle inside her until he had exploded so big and so hard he'd almost knocked her down. But she'd held him by his member with that muscle, still working him, still milking him, until he had collapsed and fallen to the barn floor.

But not only could Lily Gail never seem to get enough, she didn't seem to figure you should either. More than once Longarm had looked into that pink mouth, either one, and worried about when he would get out because she could and would hold you until she was ready to let you go. If he exploded in her vagina, she would just clamp that muscle a little tighter and keep going. If it was her mouth, she would somehow harden and tighten the rim of her lips and hold him and massage him back to life with her tongue and slowly bring him back up again. She had once made him ejaculate four times in the span of an hour, and would have gone for more if Longarm hadn't pinned her down and lain on top of her until he could get the strength back to get out of bed and put his clothes on. It made sweat start on his forehead to even think about it.

He was lifting his sleeve to wipe his forehead when he heard, "Custis! Custis! Longarm!"

He came back to himself to see Jack Shaw looking back at him and pointing. Shaw said, "Ain't that a cabin off yonder?"

Looking where Shaw pointed, Longarm was able to see the top half of a windmill and some of what looked to be a small cabin. It was about a half a mile south and east of them. It seemed to be in a little depression in the prairie, low enough that they could have missed it if they had been much further north. Longarm, still trying to come back to himself, said, "I hope to hell they have kept that windmill in good repair. These horses may not need water right now, but they damn sure will tomorrow. Especially if we are going to make any distance."

They rode slowly on toward the cabin. As they neared, Longarm felt pretty sure that it was not in use. There was no livestock in the small corral in the back, and no other sign of occupancy. The front door stood open, though the windows on both sides appeared to be boarded up against the blowing sand. This cabin, unlike the one they had used the day before, had a small roof that extended out from the front of the house, making a little porch even though the bottom was just dirt. Longarm could see an old, cane-bottomed straight-backed chair lying on its side. As they neared he could see that the blades of the windmill were turning slowly, though it was too far to tell if it was pumping water.

Shaw said, "Looks like we won't have to turn nobody out."

"Or pay rent."

They rode past the house and circled around to the back of the pen. The gate to the corral was closed. Longarm bade Shaw get down and open it while he waited. The outlaw dismounted with his hands manacled, walked over to the gate, slid a wooden bar back, and then pulled the gate outward. When it was open wide enough, the gate drooped in the sand and stuck. Shaw walked out, took his horse by the headband, and led him inside the corral, the three ponies on lead ropes following. Longarm waited until they were all inside, then rode over, took the gate in his left hand, and rode his horse into the corral, pulling the gate closed behind him. He dismounted, shoved the wooden bar home into its locked position, and turned around. Shaw was busy unbridling his horse and throwing the bridle over the fence. Longarm was gratified to see that there was water. Instead of a deep barrel, there was a long, wooden trough made out of planks. It was leaking and it was shallow, but there was water in it and all of the horses were crowding around, eager to drink. Longarm let Shaw get his saddle and saddle blanket off his horse and drape them over the fence before he said, "Jack, I reckon you better duck through the fence and walk on out there on the prairie about fifty or a hundred yards while I get the rest of these horses set up and make some kind of camp."

Shaw pulled a frown. "Aw, hell, Longarm, why can't I wait inside the cabin? It is hot as hell. I need to get in the shade. Hell, I'm about wore out. I ain't had a hell of a lot more rest than you have. Let me go in the cabin."

Longarm shook his head. "I don't know what is in the cabin. And I wouldn't be able to see you. You go on out yonder on the prairie and I'll hurry as fast as I can. Won't be long. Get you a fresh drink if you want to before you go. Or here . . ." He turned around, dug in his saddlebag, and came out with half a quart of his Maryland whiskey. "You can bite off a chunk of this while you wait." He pitched the bottle over. Shaw caught it and started through the fence.

Shaw said, "Well, hurry up. I'm starvin'. And hot. And about to go to prison. And ain't had a woman in—"

"Shut up!" Longarm commanded. "Now, get on!"

He watched as Shaw walked south a distance. Finally the man stopped, turned around, and squatted down. Longarm could see him uncork the whiskey and tilt the bottle. It made Longarm's mouth pucker a little. He'd be glad to get settled down and drink some whiskey in peace. The last week seemed to have been so rushed he hadn't been able to do anything at rest or at his own pace. Shaw had called the pace. Up until now. Now Longarm would call it for a while.

He glanced toward the sun. It was hanging low in the sky, but it was still hot enough to keep the turkey buzzards circling so high that they were mere dots. He turned to his work of getting the horses tended to and making some kind of camp.

The inside of this cabin was much like the other. The only furniture was the chair lying under the porch roof. There was a door and a window in the back, and with the ones in the front they let in enough light that he could see the place. There was a fireplace, and he was delighted to see a bundle of kindling and a few pieces of split cordwood. A fire would not only take some of the night's chill off the cabin, but it also meant they could have coffee. Longarm hadn't had any coffee since he'd left the train and headed into the mountains. But tonight he was going to drink coffee, have some kind of hot meal, smoke a cigar and drink whiskey, and get in more than a fitful two or three hours' sleep. He didn't expect Shaw to be trouble, not this early. As they got nearer and nearer to the law in New Mexico and further away from the threat of the Arizona Rangers, then yes, he might go to cutting up. But Longarm didn't figure Shaw had had much more rest and nourishment than *he* had had. Shaw might have gotten a little more whiskey drunk and a few more cigars smoked, but he had been moving just as fast to stay ahead as Longarm had trying to catch up. And Longarm hadn't had to slow himself up by murdering six of his gang either.

He went out into the corral, noting that Shaw was still squatting on the prairie, and got Shaw's bedroll and his saddlebags as well as his own. It made quite a little bundle. He also brought in his saddle blanket to use as a groundcloth. It was starting to turn into dusk. The twilight held for a long time on the high plains, but he figured he'd better get Shaw in before he got lost in the dark. He whistled and waved with his arm, signaling

Shaw to come in. He watched while the outlaw stood up and came walking forward, his arms looking awkward not swinging by his side, being positioned by his hands being manacled a foot apart. The bottle of whiskey swung from one of his hands.

Longarm opened the gate for him so he wouldn't have to climb through the fence. As he came into the corral Longarm said there was firewood and they could make coffee.

"Firewood," Shaw said. "Must have been left over since last winter. Damn sure don't see any trees around here. Yeah, coffee sounds about right. I hope you got some grub with you. I was kind of talking big about how much I had left to eat."

"I figured you might have been," Longarm said.

They went into the cabin and Longarm stacked some twigs into the little fireplace and topped that with some kindling. He struck a match on his big, square thumbnail and got the fire started. Shaw said, holding out his hands, "I reckon I'm gonna have to wear these?"

Longarm stepped back from the fireplace. He said, smiling slightly, "What would you do, Jack, if you had you for a prisoner?"

Shaw pulled a face. "I reckon I'd truss me up like a pig and keep a cocked revolver in my hand and never close an eye."

Longarm said, "It don't have to be quite that severe, Jack, but I reckon you will have to wear that iron. You and me both know you make up the rules as you go along."

Shaw laughed without humor. "Never heard it put quite like that, but I reckon you are right."

The firelight was starting to throw dancing lights around the room. Longarm knelt over his bedroll, which he used as a pack as well. He came out with a two-quart, gray, well-chipped and scorched enamel coffeepot. He handed it to Shaw. "Why don't you step on outside and fill that up with water. I'll find us some tin cups and stuff and we'll see about getting some supper on."

After the coffee water was on to boil and as the fire was simmering down, Longarm got two cans of beans out of his pack, opened them with his broad-bladed pocketknife, and put them, along with a can of tomatoes, into a small, cast-iron skillet. He took what was left of Shaw's dried beef, cut it into small pieces, added it to the beans, and then set the skillet on the hearth near the fire to warm. Before they ate, he wanted at least one cup of coffee sweetened with an equal amount of Maryland whiskey.

Shaw sat down in front of fireplace and watched him work. He said, "You're right handy around the kitchen, Miss Custis."

Longarm didn't look up. "You still got them two women you was telling me about down in Durango, Jack?"

"Yup. Wish to hell they were here right now. You wouldn't care to make a short detour, would you?"

Longarm looked up. "To where?"

Shaw shrugged. He gave a little laugh. "I was kind of kidding. Wouldn't be such a short detour."

Longarm looked at him steadily, but didn't say anything. Just then the coffee boiled over, grounds running onto the hot stones of the hearth. Longarm hooked the pot by the handle with his knife blade and pulled it back to cool some and let the grounds settle.

Shaw said, "That ought to taste pretty good."

Longarm said, "Funny how a man gets used to a few comforts. He can stand damn near anything if they are handy. Like a cup of coffee at the right time."

Shaw said abruptly, "Longarm, tell me about prison. You talked like I might have seen the inside of one when I was a lawman. I never did."

"Never delivered no prisoners to the walls?"

Shaw shook his head. "Never was called upon to do so. Just never worked out to be my job. So I ain't got the slightest idea what prison might be like."

Longarm looked into the fire. He said slowly, "Well, they ain't trying to pleasure you none, Jack, I can tell you that for sure." He looked over at his prisoner. "But then they don't send you there for singing too loud in church. So it ain't meant to be no picnic."

"Yeah, but how close do they herd you? I mean, how close are you pent up?"

Longarm frowned. He didn't want to say too much too soon. He didn't want to spook Shaw and make him harder to handle than he knew he was going to be. He said, "Well, they work you, Jack. It's hard work too. Breaking rocks, mostly. But I hear they feed you pretty good."

"Naw, that ain't what I meant. I've heard they have prison cells like we had jail cells. They got them?"

Longarm nodded. "Yeah, that's where you are when you ain't doing hard labor. Why?"

"How big are they, Longarm, them cells? They bigger than a jail cell?"

"No," Longarm said reluctantly.

"They all bars like a jail cell?"

Longarm stared into the fire. He really didn't want to answer. Shaw had already made it clear how he felt about being restricted. Even as he asked the questions Longarm could hear him breathing like he was short of breath. Longarm said, "You really want me to tell you, Jack?" He turned and looked at the outlaw.

Shaw looked nervous. He spat toward the door, which was just to his right. Then he said, shivering a little, "Getting kinda cool in here. Going to be a cold night."

Longarm was wearing a canvas ducking jacket that he'd put on after the sun had gone down. He didn't think Shaw was cold, but he said, "You got a coat in your bedroll? I'll fetch it."

Shaw shook his head. "Naw, never mind. I'm all right."

Longarm took his bandanna off to use to hold the hot handle of the coffeepot. He put two tin cups down and poured both two-thirds full of the steaming coffee. He put a little sugar in his own, something he tried not to be without, and looked questioningly at Shaw. Shaw shook his head and said, "Just that sugar that comes in a bottle. They don't let you have that in prison, do they?"

Longarm was about to raise the steaming cup to his lips. He lowered it and laughed. "Well, Jack, how'd you like to have to deal with about a thousand murderers and thieves if they was drunk?"

"I can hold my liquor," Shaw said stiffly.

"Yeah, but that ain't the point." Longarm took a deep slurp of the whiskey-loaded coffee. The whiskey had cooled it off just enough where it wouldn't burn his lips but was still plenty warm enough. He said, "Aaah! Damn, seems like I been waiting about a hundred years for that. No, Jack, the point is everybody can't hold their liquor. Besides, you got to keep it in your mind that they are aiming to punish you for what you done. Giving you whiskey ain't exactly punishment."

"I thought the idea was to lock you up where you couldn't get up to no more devilment."

Longarm shook his head. "Naw, naw. That's partly true, but it ain't all of it. When somebody comes out of prison they want to be sure he passes the word around that it is best to walk the straight and narrow rather than pack a six-by-eight cell."

Shaw was on the words instantly. "Six-foot-by-eight-foot? Is that how big they are? Or how small? Hell, that's a damn closet. I ain't sure I could stand that. Imagine being crowded in like that. Can you talk to the hombres on either side of you?"

Longarm sighed. He had not wanted to get into this with his prisoner. He said, "Not 'less you yell, Jack. The walls is pretty thick."

"Walls? You mean you're hemmed in on two sides, three sides, by walls?"

Longarm grimaced. He would have the truth. He said, "Four sides, Jack. All you got in the door is a little eyehole for the guard to look through."

Shaw was staring at him, his eyes looking strange. "And you're all jammed up in there?"

Longarm nodded. "Yeah, you and the man that shares the cell with you. Unless you're in a four-man cell. They always make the men in the cells even numbers so, say, two men can't gang up on one."

Shaw swallowed, hard, his Adam's apple bobbing up and down. His hand had started shaking so that he had to set his cup down on the dirt floor. He said, breathing rapidly, "I don't think I could take that, Custis, I don't think so at all."

Longarm looked at him, wondering if he were going to suddenly explode. He hoped not. He would surely like to have a meal in peace and finish it with whiskey and a cigar. He said soothingly, "Hell, Jack, you're a long ways from that. I get you to New Mexico, I'll try and find you the dumbest sheriff I can. Then you got to be tried. That can take months. Lot of chances to escape in there, going to and from the courthouse. Get you a good lawyer. I'd imagine you got some money in a bank somewhere. Don't go to thinking about it now. Hell, you just managed to get away from them Arizona Rangers."

Shaw looked down at his cup, and then lifted it and drank swiftly. When it was down he said, "I ain't so sure that was the best idea."

Longarm gave him a look. He didn't like the way the conversation was going. He'd pushed the skillet up closer to the fire as it had burned down, and now he could see that the beans were starting to bubble. He didn't have but one tin plate and Shaw had none. "We didn't plan to set up housekeepin'," Shaw had explained when Longarm had asked him how there couldn't be a single pan or cup or tin plate among the robbers. "If you couldn't eat it out of your hand, it was takin' up too much room. Besides, we was in kind of a hurry."

So, with a big spoon, Longarm split the beans and tomatoes and beef into two parts, putting half in the tin plate and eating out of the skillet himself. He gave Shaw the only fork he had and used the spoon. It was a little hot working out of the skillet, but Longarm made himself take it slowly, even as hungry as he was. Through a mouthful of hot beans he said, "I wish we had some light bread."

Shaw smiled with a glimmer in his eyes. "I wish I had your gun and a fast horse and you had a feather up your ass. Then we'd both be tickled."

Longarm was glad to see him coming out of his shaky-looking mood. He said, pointing at the manacles, "Those wouldn't be no hindrance to you?"

Shaw said, "Hell, Custis, you can't have everything. Didn't you know that?"

"I did. But the rate at which you been robbing folks, I wasn't sure you did."

Shaw laughed. "That's the trouble with easy money. It goes out just as easy as it goes in. You got to act big, set up drinks for the house. Bet big so you don't look like no tinhorn. Bet big long enough, you lose big."

Longarm said thoughtfully, "I'm glad to hear you figured that out."

Shaw raised his hands and jangled the chain between the cuffs. "You mean *this*? I didn't feel like I was gambling this last job, Custis. You was the wild card in the deck I hadn't counted on. Hadn't been you was on my trail, I'd still be back there in the cabin waiting for a dark night." He leaned back a little so he could see out the door of the cabin. "Moon is already starting to wane. Probably tomorrow night would have been ideal. Cross maybe an hour before dawn. Would have been black as the inside of a cow. You know this country, you know how dark it can get."

Longarm nodded. "Without a campfire you can walk ten steps from your bedroll to take a leak and never find it until morning."

"So this ain't luck. This is Custis Long."

"You asked me if I hated your guts. I reckon I ought to ask you the same thing."

"You wouldn't care either way."

Longarm shrugged. "I don't know. I never thought about it before. Most of the bandits I take in ain't as good company as you are, Jack. Most of 'em is so bone-mean, and have been all their life, they ain't had a thought for nobody but themselves in all that time. That kind of folk makes damn poor visiting company. Generally you can't wait to drop them off at the nearest jail and wash the smell of them out of your hair.''

"Well, if there was a question in there, no, I don't hate your guts. I hate it that you have to be so damn good at your job, but I ain't got nothing against you personally. Back there at the other cabin I would have killed you if I'd of had the chance. And you would have killed me.''

Longarm nodded and took a sip of coffee. His cup was nearly empty. He said, "Yeah, this is kind of a rough game we have selected to play. Got some hard rules.''

Supper was long over. Shaw had washed up their utensils, with Longarm watching from the door, and now they were sitting in front of the fireplace finishing up the coffee and both smoking cigars. Shaw had put on a leather jacket Longarm had gotten him out of his bedroll. When he'd gotten it Longarm had been glad to see that Shaw carried two blankets in addition to his canvas groundcloth. He was going to have to make his prisoner sleep outside. There was nothing in the cabin to manacle him to. The only choices were the two posts that held up the porch roof or the fence posts in the corral. Longarm wasn't too sure about the fence posts, though, as they didn't look as sturdy as the ones at the other cabin. He reckoned he'd just have to bed Shaw down under the porch roof with his arms around one of the posts. He knew the man would much rather be cuddling up to something other than a roof post, but then so would he. But he'd been too careless with Shaw already. When he'd let him unlock his manacles so he could put his leather jacket on, Longarm had stood too close. He'd seen Shaw measuring him, the manacles swinging from one hand as he'd adjusted the jacket. Longarm had casually, but immediately, taken a step backwards. Shaw

119

had smiled mockingly, and then, giving Longarm the same smile, had put his free wrist back in the cuff and clicked it into place. He hadn't said anything, but then he didn't have to.

Now Longarm told him where he was going to have to sleep. He added, "I'll get you a saddle blanket if you like. Put it down between you and your groundcloth."

Shaw shook his head. Naw. It won't be that cold. Besides, it won't be no colder out there than it will be in here. Not unless a wind comes up, and I doubt one will."

Longarm finished his coffee and carefully tamped out what was left of his cigar. He said, "Then I reckon we better get on with it. I think we had ought to make a early start. I'd like to get away from here by dawn if we can. Little before would be even better. Get some traveling done before the heat takes it out of the horses."

Shaw stood up. There was still enough light from the fire that it lit up the recesses of the cabin. He said, "I'll get my bedroll and put it down. Then you can tuck me in when you're a mind."

Longarm laid out his own bedroll against the back wall of the cabin. He put his saddle blanket down, unfolding it until it was stretched out to its four-foot-by-six-foot length. Over that he put the tarp that he rolled his blankets and the rest of his gear in. Most folks put the tarp down first and then the saddle blanket, but Longarm had never cared to lay on the salt-soaked saddle blanket, and certainly didn't want to smell it all night long. He put his two blankets down, doubling the inside one. Lastly, he set his saddle at the head to give him a sort of pillow. He could tell how cold it was the instant he got very far from the fire. There was enough split cordwood left that he could have gotten the cabin pretty warm, but it wouldn't have done Shaw any good and he didn't think it would be fair otherwise. When he was finished, he walked over to the door of the cabin. Shaw had made his bed by the eastern roof post. Longarm could see he intended to sleep on his right side with his back to the cabin. Once he was manacled around the post there wouldn't be room for him to turn over. Shaw was standing by his bedroll. He looked around as Longarm came to the door. About eight feet separated them. Longarm said, "You 'bout settled in?"

Shaw said, "I reckon."

"You want a jug of whiskey to keep you company? You got a couple bottles of your own left."

Shaw shook his head. "Naw. I've had enough. I don't know which feels worse, getting shot or riding in this sun with a head aching from whiskey. I think I'd rather be shot."

Longarm looked surprised. "I didn't know you'd been shot."

Shaw nodded. "Yeah. Wasn't a hell of a long time before I ran into you down there in Mexico." He made a little crooked smile. "It was kind of like this deal here. Only we'd robbed a bank and I didn't quite get my last partner killed. I thought the sonofabitch was dead and was walking away, and he raised up and shot me in the back."

Longarm shook his head. "Gettin' to where you can't trust nobody no more. I reckon it must not have been fatal."

"I got lucky." He dropped to his knees on his blanket, and then turned and sat down while he took his boots off. He was still wearing the leather jacket, and the combination of that and the manacles made the task of removing his boots awkward. Longarm made no move to help. It would have brought them too close. Shaw said, "I bent over to pick something up—the money, I think it was—when he fired. Bullet went in just above my shoulder blade and come out by my right collarbone. Never hit nothing serious. But don't never let nobody tell you that getting a hole bored in you is funny. Ain't a damn thing funny about it. It hurts going in and coming out and hurts while you are getting well. It was a full year before I had what I considered the natural use of my right arm and hand. I could use them, but they was just a kind of little hitch in it. That scar tissue, you know.''

"Yeah, I know," Longarm said slowly. "I'm not much of a one for getting shot myself. Though I'd rather have it hurt than not feel anything."

Shaw laughed. "Yeah, I know about that. No, I reckon I can wait for that sensation."

"Or the lack of it."

"Yeah."

"You need anything else? You going to sleep in that jacket?"

"I reckon to."

"Well, you won't be movin' around much, so I don't reckon it will bind you. Look here."

Longarm took a step toward Shaw and pitched the key to him. Shaw caught it in the air, and Longarm watched as he unlocked one of the manacles and then passed the end around the post. Longarm took another step toward Shaw, and leaned to watch the outlaw put the cuff around his left wrist. Longarm said, "You ain't got to make it pinch, Jack, but I want to see that cuff snugged up and hear it click at least twice."

Shaw smiled slightly. "I ain't likely to break these." Still on his knees he raised both his hands, the chain encircling the post. "You want to check them?"

"Naw," Longarm said. "I imagine you'd like for me to forget to ask for the key back, but I believe you just put it into your jacket pocket."

Shaw faked an astonished look. "Why, my goodness, did I do that?" He swiveled his body around until he could reach into the side pocket of his jacket. He came out holding a key so Longarm could see it.

Longarm said, "Pitch it as best you can toward the end of your blankets."

In an awkward move, with his hands restricted by the manacles, Shaw transferred the key to his left hand and then pitched it toward Longarm. It landed at the foot of the blankets. Longarm bent down, watching Shaw, and retrieved the key.

Shaw laughed. "You looked like you thought I was gonna jump you. Hell, Longarm, I ain't much of a threat to nobody."

"Can you get in your bed all right?"

"Yeah," Shaw said. While Longarm watched, he pawed around with his stocking feet and worked them under his two blankets, gradually easing his body down under his covers. Shaw said, "Yeah, I'm fine."

Longarm turned. "You holler at me if you're first awake. I don't reckon you got any more interest than I do hanging around in these parts."

"If it hadn't of been for the horses and the water situation, I'd of been willing to of kept on riding."

Longarm sat down on his bedroll inside the cabin and took off his boots. The fire was down now so that it just provided a little glow in the room. But there was still good moonlight, and enough streamed in through the two doors and three windows that the interior of the cabin was clear enough. Longarm had placed his bedding so that he could see through the door and see most of Shaw. He didn't reckon the man was going anywhere, but still, he never slept too well in the company of bandits, even when they were manacled to part of the house.

Before he settled down, he took his rifle and hid it under the blankets between himself and the wall. He pulled his gunbelt off, withdrew his revolver, and snuggled it up under his saddle. For anyone to get at his weapons they would have to disturb him. There were the other weapons, still together with the rest of Shaw's stuff, but they were all unloaded and the ammunition hidden in Shaw's saddlebags. Longarm would have hidden them in his own, but his bags were full. It didn't make much difference. If Shaw somehow got loose while Longarm was sleeping, the outlaw could brain him with a length of cordwood. He could then arm himself at leisure.

Longarm shucked off his canvas jacket and threw it over his bed against the wall. Finally, now feeling the cold, he loosened his belt, took his hat off, and slipped down between his blankets. He'd placed a bottle of whiskey to hand, and he had a good pull off of that before he got all the way laid out with just part of his head resting on his saddle. It felt good to be stretched out and warm. It felt good after all the hard, anxious going to know that the chase was finally coming to an end. If they rode hard they should be in New Mexico Territory by the next evening. Whether or not they'd be close enough to a town big enough for him to surrender Shaw in, Longarm couldn't say. He'd need to look at a map or ask someone.

He was not ordinarily a man who had much trouble going to sleep, but this night his mind wouldn't settle down. He knew he'd played the Rangers false by not leaving them any kind of sign, but he'd told Shaw if he'd surrender he'd take him to New Mexico. With the conditions as they were and the position he was in, he didn't see where he had had any choice. He hadn't known for certain when the Rangers were coming, and he sure as hell hadn't known how long he could hold out. So he'd made the best deal he could, and part of that deal had been to keep his word about taking Shaw to New Mexico Territory. And he couldn't have done that if he'd left the Rangers clear sign. It was, he reckoned, a kind of moral and legal standoff.

With that straight in his mind, he shut his eyes and began to relax. In a few moments he was deeply asleep.

Chapter 8

Longarm came awake to the sound of his name being called from someplace near and the light tapping of something hard against his forehead. He opened his eyes slowly, but moved no other part of him. When he could focus, he saw Jack Shaw squatting on the cabin floor right at his head with a revolver in his hand. He took care to note that the pistol was cocked but Shaw didn't have his finger resting on the trigger.

Shaw said, "You better get up, Longarm. My hells, but you can sleep. Somebody is gonna slip up on you in the night and do you a harm you keep on sleeping that deep. Sleeping like a dead man, and for a damn good reason."

Longarm said, still not moving, "You want me to sit up or just prezactly what?"

Shaw stood up and moved back, keeping the muzzle of the pistol covering Longarm. He said, "Yeah, sit up and sling the blankets back."

Longarm did so, being careful to make his movements slow and deliberate. Right then he had a lot of questions, but he didn't reckon it was the time to ask them. He could see that the inside of the cabin was bright. At first, when he'd opened his eyes, he'd thought it was because dawn had come. But he could see now that Shaw had built up a pretty good fire in the cabin. Longarm could see through the front door that it was almost black dark outside, which meant that the moon was down and dawn wasn't far off. He glanced toward the fireplace. He could see that the coffeepot had been used and was sitting back from the fire a little. It looked as if it had been placed to keep the contents hot, but not to boil over. He said, "What now?"

Shaw chuckled. "You seem to understand this business pretty well, Custis. What do you reckon is the next step?"

Longarm thought, probably walk me out in the dark and put a bullet in my head. But he didn't voice the thought or give Shaw any other ideas. He said, "I don't know. It's dealer's choice and you got the cards." He was studying the revolver in Shaw's hand. It wasn't one of his. It had ivory grips. He'd never cared for a gun with white on it. Unhandy in the dark. It might not give you away, but why take the chance. That meant that, maybe, Shaw hadn't found his gun under the saddle.

Shaw said, "I'm going to let you take my place on the front porch. Unfortunately, I done took my blankets up so you'll be sitting in the dust."

Now he could see that Shaw had the set of manacles in his left hand. They'd been dangling down by his leg, out of sight. He could see that both jaws were open. He didn't know how, but Shaw had somehow managed to open the cuffs. Maybe Longarm had been careless in checking and Shaw hadn't really closed the cuffs around his wrists. But no, if he'd simply left them too loose so he could slip his hands out, then the jaws wouldn't be open. No, they had been unlocked. But how or by who, Longarm couldn't understand.

"You mind if I put my boots on?"

Shaw laughed. "I reckon we'll hold up on the boots for a bit. You seem to know a good deal about boots and pistols. I wouldn't be surprised if you had one in your boot. I'll check them when I get you settled down and pitch them to you if they are all right. Move on out there now. It'll be cold at first, but dawn ain't far off. I got to get moving. So I would appreciate it if you would move along pretty fast. I seen you eyeing that coffee and I'll fetch you some. Yeah, I've had time to make coffee and build a fire. Like I say, Longarm, I'm surprised you're alive the way you sleep."

Longarm said grimly, "Me too."

He walked carefully out into the cold dark and stopped at the eastern porch post. A rectangle of light was cast out the front door onto the dirt of the porch floor. The right-hand corner of it illuminated the post. Longarm stopped and looked back at Shaw. "What next?"

"Either sit down or get down on yore knees. You are gonna cuff yoreself to that post. You ought to be familiar with how that works."

Longarm sat down. He could feel the short hairs at the back of his neck bristling. Shaw was a killer, a man who would put a bullet in your brain on a whim. If Longarm was going to get shot, he'd rather not have it from the back with his hands manacled. He looked around at the outlaw. "Jack," he said, "if you're a mind to shoot me, I'd druther take it in the chest standing up."

Shaw laughed. "Hell, don't tell me the great Longarm is afraid. I thought you was supposed to be copper-plated and bullet-proof. Hell! You mean you put your boots on just like the rest of us?"

He gave Jack Shaw a level, hard look. "I can't stop you from shooting me, Jack, but I don't need your mouth all over it."

Shaw gave a bark of laughter. "Hell, Longarm, I ain't gonna kill you. You might die here, but I ain't gonna put a bullet in you. You played square with me, and I ain't gonna put a hole in you for your troubles. You would have been within yore rights back yonder yesterday in sayin' it was no deal when I couldn't produce the money. But you didn't. You kept your end up. I have friendly feelings for you, Custis, believe it or not. That is mighty unusual for me. I hope you don't come to no harm. Now here. Catch this.''

Longarm caught the manacles by the chain as they flew toward him. He was sitting with his legs under him facing the post. He put one of the open jaws over his right wrist and closed it, hearing the ratcheting sound as it closed up. It was still loose on his wrist.

Shaw said, grinning, ''I want to hear them clicks, Custis. You know how to do that thing. I want to see you shove that ratchet home. I believe that cuff on your right wrist needs about one more click. She looks a mite loose. Might chafe you and we can't have that.''

Longarm took his left hand and squeezed the cuff until the ratchet was pushed into the lock one more notch. The click was audible.

''Now yore left hand,'' Shaw said. ''Get a move on, Longarm.''

With his right hand he encircled his left wrist with the opened cuff, and then closed it down until he could feel it all the way around on his wrist. He said, ''That satisfy you?''

''Yeah,'' Shaw said. He shoved his revolver home into its holster. For the first time Longarm noticed that Shaw had his gunbelt on. He'd never seen the man wearing it because Longarm had had him drop it before he was allowed to come out of the cabin when he surrendered. Shaw was also wearing his leather coat. The outlaw said, ''Custis, I'll bring you some coffee and a bottle of whiskey, but I got to know where your revolver and your rifle are. I ain't going to shoot you, but I ain't going to leave it so you'll shoot me either. I've got the rest of the guns and gear nearly packed up. I don't want to have to search the cabin, Custis, so don't make nothing out of this.''

Longarm spat. His mouth was dry from breathing the high plains air all night. He said, ''My revolver is in my saddlebag, the one facing the head of my bed. My rifle is under my blankets up close to the wall. And I'd appreciate some water if you can manage it."

Shaw said, "This ought to not take long. When I'm done I'll have a cup of coffee with you and then I'll be on the trail."

He was back quickly with one of the water bags. It had better than a gallon of water in it, and it was awkward for Longarm to get the top up to his mouth. Shaw reached out a hand and helped him.

"You got it?"

"Yeah," Longarm said. "I can manage it."

"I got to get ready."

Shaw disappeared back into the cabin while Longarm drank. When he was finished, he lowered the bag carefully and screwed the cap back onto the bag. The cap was attached to the bag by a little chain so it wouldn't get lost. He glanced toward the doorway, listening to Shaw rustling around. Half bemused, he wondered if Shaw knew Longarm had two revolvers and that one was hidden under his saddle and the other, the one with the nine-inch barrel, was in his saddlebag. It really wasn't anything to speculate about, not so long as he was chained to the post. He wondered if Shaw was going to tell him how he'd gotten out of the manacles. Longarm felt that he would. He knew that Shaw considered himself just a touch smarter than everyone else, and he didn't think the man could pass up a chance to gloat. Whatever he had done had been slick because Longarm couldn't think of a single way out of the manacles. Shaw didn't have hands as big as his, but he still didn't slip them out. Longarm tried pushing up against the ratchet with his thumbs, but he might as well have been trying to move a mountain with a mule. The manacles were solid.

Shaw came back out. He was carrying a cup of steaming coffee in either hand and had a bottle of whiskey under his arm. He set one tin cup on the ground where Longarm could reach it and stood the bottle of whiskey next to it.

"There," he said, "that ought to be some comfort."

"Thanks," Longarm said. He unplugged the bottle of whiskey and poured a little in his cup. He didn't want too much. As Shaw had said, having a whisky head under a hot sun was not very pleasant. Longarm lifted his cup and took a sip. "Aaaah," he said, "ain't nothing like a cup of coffee when you have just lost your prisoner and are sitting in his handcuffs."

Shaw laughed. He had gone and fetched the chair that had been lying on its side and brought it back and set it a few feet from Longarm. He said, "Yeah, Custis, you may wish I'd of shot you. This ain't gonna look too good back at marshal headquarters, wherever that might be. Denver, ain't it?"

Longarm nodded. "I guess you are going to make me ask you and then you might not answer, but I'd give a pretty penny to know how you got out of these cuffs."

Shaw smiled, enjoyment dancing in his eyes. He said, "I reckon you would, Custis. But would you tell if you was me? Ain't that what you're always askin' me?"

Longarm shrugged. "It don't matter. Probably something simple I just overlooked. You having been a town marshal, you probably had a good deal more experience with these things than me, Saturday night drunks and such. I don't reckon I've used these damn things a half-dozen times since I got 'em. Don't usually need them."

Shaw looked indignant at the idea that his law work had mainly involved taking town drunks to jail. He said, "I don't know a damn bit about them that you don't know yourself! And I reckon I handled a few rough customers that wasn't drunk myself."

Longarm said, protesting, "Hell, Jack, it don't matter. I was curious is all."

Shaw took a drink of his coffee. "I'm going to tell

you." He slapped his knee and let out a bark of laughter. "Because I want to see the look on your face. It was slick, Custis, mighty slick."

"I would reckon it was if you pulled it off."

Shaw leaned forward, putting his elbows on his knees. "Custis, it was a piece of luck beyond what I could imagine. Back when I was in law I carried a set of manacles just like you, in my saddlebags. And carried the key in my right-hand pants pocket. You know the size of them things. They ain't so big they bother you, but you are aware of them there in your pocket."

Longarm said dryly, "Keeps you from getting confused about which is your right and which is your left."

"You want to hear this or not?"

Longarm smiled and sipped at his coffee.

"Anyway, over the eight, nine years I got used to carrying that key in my pocket. It was like it was a good-luck piece or something. Besides, I wasn't sure but it might not come in handy someday. You ever notice that a key will open more than one set? Especially when they get older?"

Longarm didn't say anything, just sipped at his coffee.

"Well, when they get older and the notches get the edge off them, you can damn near open a pair with the head of a horseshoe nail. You remember back at the other cabin how I kept carrying on, asking you how you was going to truss me up? Was you going to bind me, tie my hands together? I said I couldn't stand it. Well, that part is true. I can't stand having my hands tied behind me. I can't stand to be constrained."

Longarm nodded. "So you used your key to open them. Hell, I couldn't have seen that coming. I searched you, but for weapons." He shrugged. "My mistake."

"Naw, naw, naw. That wasn't the way of it at all. After I'd surrendered and you'd thrown me them manacles to put on, my heart sank. Hell, they looked brand-new, like they hadn't been used. And now you tell me they was. Or at least very seldom used. Well, that scared me to death. My whole plan had been that I'd be able to unlock your manacles when you chained me up for the night. I knew you was as wore out as I was and that you wouldn't be sleeping so light."

"Wait a minute," Longarm said. "What if I hadn't been going to manacle you? What if I'd had to bind your hands?"

Shaw shook his head. "Then I'd of never surrendered. I'd of waited until I saw them Rangers coming, and then I would have taken my chances with a break on a horse. I know what kind of shot you are, Longarm, and I know odds would have been against me, but that would have been a choice over the way them Rangers would have treated me. I'd of waited as long as I could, letting you get whipped down by that sun and lack of water. Then I'd of bunched the horses and tried it that way in one bolt."

Longarm frowned. "Then where in hell did you get the key if you didn't use the one you had?"

"Let me tell this my own way. Last night, when you got my leather coat and let me get it on, I managed to get my key out of my pants pocket and into the right-hand pocket of my coat. Last night, when you brought me out here to chain me up to the post, you pitched me the key so I could unlock my left manacle and get my arms around the post. I made a big business out of making it look like I was being cute and hiding the key in my pocket. I wasn't. I was switching keys. The key I throwed back to you was mine. You went to bed leaving me with the key to those there manacles in easy reach in my coat pocket."

Longarm nodded unhappily. "Well, congratulation, Jack, you made a damn fool out of me. I reckon this is what comes of breaking regulations like I done. Saying I would take you to New Mexico when I should have held you for the Rangers."

"Aw, hell, Longarm. Don't take on about it. With your record, what is one little mistake going to amount to?"

Longarm said grimly, "Quite a bit." He motioned with his head. "Up here where I am supposed to do my thinking."

"By the way, I reckon you better stand up. Set your coffee down, this won't take a minute." Shaw stood up, took his revolver out of the holster, and laid it on the seat of his chair. He came at Longarm from the back as the marshal stood up. First he patted Longarm's pants pockets, and then the pockets in his shirt. He found the cartridges in Longarm's right-hand shirt pocket. He said, "What's this? Ammunition? Longarm, that ain't going to do you much good." He dug down into the pocket, pulled out the bullets, and threw them off into the prairie. It was still too dark for Longarm to see where they went.

Shaw said, "Where is that other key, Longarm?"

Longarm jerked his head toward the cabin. "In my saddlebags. I forget which side." He said the lie easily and smoothly.

"I didn't see it when I went looking for your revolver."

Longarm shrugged. "That's where I always put it. Look around on the floor beside them. I might have missed the mouth. I never carry nothing in my pockets besides that jackknife which is in by the fireplace. Stuff bothers me in my front pockets. Pants legs are too tight."

Shaw said, stepping back, "Well, it don't really matter." He picked up his revolver and sat back down, shoving the pistol home in its holster. "I ain't leaving you a gun even if you could get loose. Besides, I'll be long gone."

"Where you headed, Jack? Mexico?"

"By and by. First I'm going to notch back by the cabin and pick up my winnings from that train."

Longarm gave him a quick glance. "Cabin?"

Shaw gave a small laugh. "Did I say cabin? I meant canyon. Canyon, like I told you. In that pile of rocks."

Longarm kept his eyes on the face of the outlaw. He felt pretty sure that he himself wasn't the only one doing some hard and fast lying. He said, "I'd figure you wouldn't head toward that part of the country. Liable to be working alive with Arizona Rangers."

Shaw shook his head. "I don't reckon now. I reckon they would have found no sign from you, other than them two dead horses, and headed due south in hot pursuit figuring me to be running for the border. Why would they hang around there?"

"You talking about the canyon or the cabin?"

Shaw frowned. "Why, either one. Besides, what difference does it make if I run across them. I'll be coming from the southeast. They won't be looking for me."

Longarm nodded toward Shaw's face. "There is that birthmark, Jack. It's a dead giveaway."

Shaw touched his face. "Hell, I figure whiskers is hiding that cursed thing by now. I ain't shaved in a week. Can you see it?"

"It's too dark to tell. Besides, I know it's there." He changed the subject. "Let me ask you something, Jack. You claim if I hadn't been going to manacle you that you'd of never surrendered. Now, truth be told, wasn't you gettin' a little pent up in that cabin? Way you tell it, you don't like to be crowded, and I had you where you couldn't go out the back or the front."

Shaw reached up and rubbed the whiskers on his neck as he thought. He finally said, "Yeah, they is some truth to that. I can't stand that feeling, and you was pressing me pretty close. But I think I'd of broke for it before I surrendered. I was balanced on a knife blade anyways. But I figured on a two-day ride after you made the offer about New Mexico. I figured I'd have a chance to get loose from you. I know your reputation and all, but I was counting on that key."

134

"So it wasn't just the thought of the Rangers made you decide to surrender."

Shaw nodded. "Not altogether. I never figured to see the inside of prison if that is what you are asking. But now let me ask you something."

"What?"

Shaw hesitated for a moment. By the light of the fire still coming through the door Longarm could see something in Shaw's face he couldn't identify. It looked a little like uncertainty, and a little like fear. But Shaw didn't have any reason to feel either of those. Finally Shaw said, "You talked about men you'd brought to bay running at your gun. Are you talking about men that knew you?"

"What do you mean, knew me?"

"Aw, hell, Custis, you know damn good and well what I mean. Did they know it was you, the famous damn Longarm? The dead shot? Quit acting modest. Did they charge at you with any hope of overcoming you or getting past you? In other words, did they know it was a sure thing they was going to get killed?"

"You mean, was they executing themselves after passing judgment? Yeah. I'd have to say they knew what was going to happen. As to that famous stuff and the dead shot, I don't know. They didn't stop to give me their opinions on the matter. What the hell are you so interested for? Ain't got a damn thing to do with you. Last time you felt guilty was when you had to pay a whore full price." Longarm suddenly shivered.

"What's the matter with you? You feel somebody walk over your grave?"

"Hell, Jack, it's cold. Or ain't you noticed?"

"You want me to get your jacket?"

Longarm said quickly, "No!" Then, realizing that Shaw might have read something into his quick refusal, he said, "Can't get the damn jacket on without taking off the cuffs, and then I'd be stuck in it when the sun commences to blaze. You might hang one of

135

my blankets over my shoulders. I'd be obliged for that.''

He turned his head and watched Shaw go into the cabin. He didn't want Shaw going anywhere near the jacket with the key in the pocket. It was the wrong key, but it was the only key he had. And besides, maybe Shaw was right. Maybe one key fit more than one set of manacles.

Shaw came back and threw the blanket over Longarm's shoulders. He said, ''Well, ol' partner, I reckon this is where we fork trails. It is getting on for dawn and I better get to moving.''

Longarm said, ''I can't believe you are heading back in the direction of them Rangers.''

''Believe it. Believe it about sixty thousand dollars worth.''

''I think you lied to me, Jack. I think that money was there at the cabin all the time. Though I'm damned if I know where unless you buried it, but I didn't see no shovel.''

Shaw said, ''Look at it this way, Custis. All in all, what the hell difference does it make to you?''

Longarm shrugged. ''None, I reckon. Except I always had a natural curiosity.''

''It didn't kill you this time. But I'd try and keep it in check was I you.'' Shaw came over and dropped two cigars and a half-dozen matches. He said, ''I wish you good luck, Custis. I'm leaving two horses in the corral. I'm even leaving your saddle and gear. They'd just slow me up.''

Longarm said, ''You know, Jack, if somebody don't come along I ain't going to last long like this. Two, maybe three or four days.''

Shaw nodded. ''I know it. Tell you what. When I get where I'm going I'll wire the nearest sheriff where you are. Maybe they'll get to you in time and maybe they won't.''

''I don't hold it against you, Jack. We both know how the game is played. You are on the run. I'm just amazed you didn't put a bullet in my ear.''

"I would have if I hadn't had no other choice. But I think this will slow you up long enough for me to get my business done. I'll be taking off now, Custis. I hope we don't see each other again. Not where business is concerned. Maybe you'll take another vacation in Mexico and we'll meet up.''

"You take it easy, Jack.''

"Yeah, *adios*.''

After a while Longarm heard the muffled sounds of hoofbeats, softened by the sand, receding into the distance. Only then did he realize how tightly he'd been holding himself. He slowly relaxed down on to the ground. "Damn!'' he said aloud. "Boy, howdy!''

Given the situation, he would have never believed that Jack Shaw would have ridden off and left him alive. He'd been expecting a bullet with every word, with every move, with every second. But then, what made a man like Jack Shaw so dangerous was his unpredictability. As a last gesture Shaw had brought the coffeepot out, still half full, before he left. With an awkward hand, because of the manacles, Longarm poured his cup half full and then added a little of the whiskey. The coffee would be weak, second grounds, since Shaw had just added water to what was left in the pot and let it simmer some more. But that was all right. It was good and warm and felt good going down his gullet. He hadn't been afraid as much as he had dreaded the thought of being shot while manacled to a post. And then to be found like that. It wasn't the way he wanted to go at all. Not that he'd ever selected a good way, or a way he thought would be best. There was no best, just a few ways that were better than it being clear he had been taken off his guard and manacled with his own cuffs and then killed. It wouldn't have looked good on his record, he thought wryly to himself.

He wasn't at all certain how he was going to get out of the manacles. He had some hope for the key he hoped still resided in his jacket pocket, but he had to find some way of getting loose from the post before he could worry about the key. And until it got lighter he wasn't going to be able to examine the situation very well. The fire from inside was dying out and casting less and less light and less and less warmth. He was grateful for the blanket over his shoulders. It didn't help all of him, but it at least kept his back warm.

The whiskey and coffee kept his insides in good shape, though he had no plans to drink much of the whiskey. He settled down to wait for dawn, not sure himself how far off it was.

As it had before, it came light all of a sudden. Longarm thought he would never cease to be amazed by the sunrises and sunsets in the high plains. There was something about them that clearly let you know a mighty hand was in charge, and if not a hand, then a design that was intended to let you know just about how small you were, no matter what size shirt you wore.

He guessed Shaw might have been gone an hour, but no more, maybe even less. As soon as he could see, Longarm began the task of freeing himself by examining the roof post he was chained to. It appeared to be a piece of mountain cedar, some six inches in thickness. He thumped it up and down with his knuckles, and pretty well convinced himself the post was solid and likely to remain so for another hundred years or so.

To study the base he pulled his hands down, got down on his knees, and put his face close to the end of the post. If it was buried in the ground, he didn't have much chance. But as near as he could tell, and from what he could see by scraping away at the rock-hard dirt around the bottom of the post, it was just sitting on the ground and not buried. Next, he looked up to the end of the post where it supported the roof. The end was against the beam that ran all the way across at the edge of the porch. Longarm could not see a single nail or screw or even a piece of wire holding the post and the beam together. The post was simply held in place by the weight of the roof and the post kept the roof supported. It was not a lash-up that was intended for the fancy. It was only intended as a place for a cowboy to sit of a hot afternoon and look out over the prairie from the shade.

He looked the roof over. It was made up of fairly heavy sawn beams that formed a framework that had then been covered with tin. The back end of the roof was held to the face of the building by what looked to Longarm, glancing upward and leaning as far back as he could, like tin straps that had somehow been secured to the rock face, maybe by long screws into the mortar between the stones.

He sat down and took his boot off. It was a hard job working with the manacles on. His plan was to try and lift the post and then, while he held it an inch off the ground, slide his boot tip in under it. Then, with the base of the post held off the ground enough for the chain to pass under, he'd get down on the ground, slide the chain under until he got to his boot tip, and then yank himself free. He had no idea if it would work or not.

He rested a few minutes, thinking about it, and then stood up and got himself in position. He hugged the post to him and carefully curled his arms around the wood. He could feel how slick it was, how the weather and the sand had smoothed it down. Once, probably, it had had bark on it, but that was long since worn away. The post was a little bent, but the kink was too high up for him to make use of. He had to get hold of it around his belt or a little below to bring his powerful back and leg muscles into play. Nobody was going to lift the post and that part of the roof with just arm muscles.

He set himself, feeling for his grip. He could feel his heart beating. If this didn't work, he didn't know what he was going to do. He tightened his hands and then his arms around the post, pulling it to him, to his chest, locking it solid. Slowly he began to lift. He could feel the post start to come, feel it part with the dirt. He strained harder and harder, his teeth gritted, his eyes closed, the sweat popping out on his forehead. Then, just as he thought the post was about to come up some more, his hands began to slip. Frantically he hugged the post harder and harder, desperately trying to force it to rise.

Then, all of a sudden, he gave out. He collapsed to his knees, panting, his breath coming in gasps. For a long few moments he stayed that way. Finally he straightened up and sat down heavily. He looked up at the underside of the roof. It appeared to him that the top of the post had moved slightly from its centered position on the end beam. He didn't know what that meant, but at least something had happened besides him almost ruining his back.

He stayed down on the ground, studying the post, studying the roof, trying to think of some way to get a piece of chain through a solid piece of wood. He even eyed the matches Shaw had left him, wondering if he could somehow set the wood framework on fire and burn the thing down. But the roofing was tin and the boards of the framework were too far apart to burn. If the roof had been shingled with wood shakes, he wouldn't have hesitated for a moment.

Finally he looked at the chair Shaw had been sitting in and then up at the roof. The front edge of the roof was low. He'd noticed, going and coming under it, that he'd had to duck his head when he was wearing his hat. He stood up and looked at a beam running from the wall to the front edge of the roof. It looked to be a two-by-six plank. It was the beam the top of the post was abutted against. When he stood up, it was only some six to eight inches over his head. He glanced again at the chair, which he reckoned to be about thirty-four or thirty-six inches high at the seat. It was, he thought, worth a try.

He sat down again, and then lay down and wiggled and squirmed on his back toward the chair, until he could just reach one of the legs with the toes of his stocking foot. He curled his big toe around the leg, and then slowly and carefully dragged it toward him. The chair came until he could get his whole foot behind the leg, and he gave a jerk and the chair came flying to him.

140

Slowly he worked his way back up to a sitting position, and then circled the post until he was out from under the roof. He pulled the chair up until the seat was just touching the post on the cabin side. He worked his way back around and, with some difficulty, picked up his blanket, folded it, and then refolded it and then folded it again until it was a good pad some six inches thick. With both hands he carefully placed it over his right shoulder and across his neck. It would accomplish two things; it would give him some added height and it would serve as a pad between his shoulder and back and the hard two-by-six.

Before he did anything else, he sat down in the chair and carefully drew his boot back on his right foot. The extra two inches in height might make the difference.

Now was the test, and if it didn't work he didn't know what he was going to do. He stood up and put one boot on the edge of the chair. It was a cane-bottomed chair, so he couldn't use the middle. But the back and the frame were made out of the same tough mountain cedar as the post, and he figured it would stand the strain. Holding on to the post with both hands, he positioned his right foot on the right-hand edge of the chair and slowly stepped up, putting his left boot on the other side of the seat. He was moving cautiously so as not to dislodge the blanket over his shoulder.

As he stood up slowly he felt his back and shoulder come into contact with the roof beam with his body still not straight. He calculated that, if he could and if the chair didn't break, he ought to be able to raise the roof at least two or three inches. If he had the strength. But at least he'd be using his biggest muscles, in his back and in his legs.

He gave himself a moment to get positioned, feeling around for the most comfortable position for his shoulder against the beam. He moved his boots around, trying to get them as near the legs as possible. He figured he had about one try. The chair could break and give way, he could hurt himself trying to lift such a load, or the nails in the roof could give. If any of those events happened he was finished.

When he was ready, he took hold of the post with both his hands, bent his knees as he slowly straightened his body, and made firm contact with the beam across his shoulder and the top of his back. He closed his eyes and concentrated all his attention into straightening his legs. If the roof cleared the post by a fraction of an inch he would whip his hands up and pull the chain through the opening.

He put a strain on his legs, letting it gradually run up his body to his shoulder. Nothing moved. It felt like he was pushing against solid rock. He willed his legs to push harder. And then harder still. He heard the chair creak alarmingly. Still there was no movement. He could feel the sweat pop out all over his face. His teeth were gritted so hard they must surely crack. He could feel the blood rushing to his face. Still he pushed harder. The chair gave an agonizing shriek as if it were being tortured. His feet felt as if they were going flat in his boots.

The roof moved.

It was very slight, but he had felt it give a little. He summoned every last desperate ounce of strength he had. The roof moved slightly more. His eyes were squinted so that he couldn't quite see the separation between the post and the beam. With a last gasp he surged upwards against the roof in a desperate attempt to be free.

He suddenly felt pressure against the chain. The post was starting to fall outwards. If he didn't quickly get his hands up and pull the chain through, the post would fall outward but stay hung against his chain, and then, for added trouble, the roof would fall on him as he tried to get down.

With his body starting to fail, with his legs trembling, with his neck and back screaming with pain, he made one swift, desperate move, jerking the chain up and toward himself. He felt it come through some kind of opening. He couldn't see it. His eyes felt as if they were filled with blood. And then part of the chair broke with a loud crack and the next thing Longarm knew he was falling backwards. As he fell he saw the porch roof following him. He tried, desperately, in midair, to turn so that he wouldn't land full on his back. But then he hit; the breath jolted out of his lungs as he landed hard. Before he went unconscious as his head hit the hard dirt of the porch floor, he had a view of the porch roof continuing to descend, threatening to drop a ton of wood and tin and nails and dust on top of his aching, challenged body.

Chapter 9

How long he was out, he had no idea. All he knew was that he came to with a splitting headache and the sight of the right half of the porch roof hanging down within a yard of the ground. The post that had formerly held it up was lying out in the yard where it had fallen.

For a long few moments he lay still without moving, trying to feel his body, wondering if anything was broken. This was no country to break a leg or a hip or anything else that would leave you unable to mount a horse, much less catch one and saddle it.

He gazed along the length of his body and saw his bottle of whiskey lying overturned. So was the coffeepot. Further on, the chair lay on its side. The right leg appeared to have broken at a knot halfway down its length. He thought, inanely, that he was getting good at making three-legged chairs. He'd been in two line cabins and he'd made three-legged chairs out of all the available furniture. Come fall, the returning line riders were going to wonder who'd been assaulting their sitting material.

The roof gave a groan and seemed to settle a little more. It brought Longarm alert. Ignoring his body's aches and complaints, he quickly reached in and grabbed his coffeepot and cup and the bottle of whiskey, and then scuttled backwards into the doorway of the cabin. Surprisingly enough, the blanket was still on his shoulder, though it was now draped like a serape. He knew he hurt, but he wouldn't let his mind think about it. He uncorked the whiskey and had a long, medicinal pull. He gasped when he took the bottle away from his mouth. He didn't normally take that much down at a time, but he knew he was going to need it to oil up his joints and shoulder and back, which he was pretty sure was broken.

He looked down at the manacles on his wrists. If he had to he could operate while wearing them, but he was hopeful that the key in his canvas jacket pocket would unlock them. If not, he'd have to find a town with a blacksmith and get the smith to just cut the chain. It would be inconvenient, but he could do his work.

He sat there. He felt a swelling desire to get on Shaw's trail, take after him while the scent was still hot, but he couldn't make himself move. He looked up at the porch roof. Fully half of it was now drooping down, the right corner no more than a foot off the ground. He was amazed at what he had lifted. Individually the parts didn't weigh much, but connected, they came to a sizeable amount. He shook his head and shuddered, very glad to be free from the post. He didn't stop to think what he would have done if he hadn't gotten loose. He didn't want to think about that. As near as he could tell, the remote cabin wasn't on the way to anywhere, and he could have been there until he cured in the sun. Shaw had said he would telegraph back to a sheriff, but whether he would have or not was open to question. As was whether or not some sheriff would have ridden fifty miles on the dubious validity of a telegram.

He was about to get up, dreading it, when he happened to glance down at the right side of his right boot. It had split. Where the leather of the boot was sewn to the sole, the stitching had broken. He could see little tufts of it sticking up from his sole. He could wiggle his right toe and see it move through the split. "Damn!" he said aloud.

There was nothing for it but to get up and see if the key fit. If it didn't, then it was saddle a horse and take off with his hands a foot apart. He rolled over and came to his feet. For a second he swayed and little white spots danced in front of his eyes. He stayed still, willing all the parts of his body to take control. After a second the dizziness passed. He took a step and felt like his hips were breaking. "Damn!" he said aloud, driving the word through his gritted teeth.

The next step wasn't any easier, nor the next. He said aloud, "Hell, I feel two inches shorter. Maybe three. Maybe four."

He could feel the pain as a constant, beginning in his right shoulder, jumping over to his backbone, and then spreading downward all the way through his hips, then down to his knees, and finally to his ankles and feet. "What a job," he said wearily. "But it shore beats working."

He made it to his blankets, and then eased himself to the ground. For a moment he sat very still, letting the pain do its best, letting the pain just go ahead and consume him as he relaxed his body into it. He had learned a long time ago that you only made matters worse if you tried to fight pain. If you tried that, all you did was stiffen up and make your muscles rigid, and wear yourself out in the fight. And it was a useless fight because the pain was going to win no matter what you did. The best way to handle it was to sit back and let it come, accommodate yourself to it. That way, after a while, it got to be a part of you so that you didn't notice it so much anymore. But you had to be willing to be patient and sit there and relax and get used to it. It didn't make it hurt any less, but after a while you got so you didn't notice it so much.

He took another hard hit off the bottle, but did it slowly and resolutely. He was very conscious that he had many hours ahead of him with the sun beating down on his head. That, at least, was a good thing. The sun might not do him any other good, but it would at least bake some of the hurt out of his bones and muscles and joints.

Finally he reached back over his blankets, got his canvas jacket, and dragged it to him. The key was still in the right-hand pocket. It was a round steel key with teeth on the end and little wings to turn it with. It was about the size of a pistol cartridge. In the dim light he could see numbers die-stamped on the side of the key. He looked for a matching set on the manacles. There was a set of numbers, but they didn't match those on the key. He contemplated the keyhole in his left manacle. It was a round little hole with notches that hopefully matched the teeth on the round little key. Hopefully he stuck the key into the hole. It fit. He tried turning the key to the left. Nothing happened. He frowned. With not much optimisim he turned the key to the right. It went halfway around and he felt something click inside the manacle releasing the ratchets. He felt the cuff come loose. "I'll be damned," he said. He opened the cuff and removed his left hand. To the inside of the little cabin he said, "What the hell they put numbers on 'em for if they all fit the same?"

With confidence he transferred the key to his left hand and tried the right cuff. The key went into the hole with no trouble, but nothing happened no matter which way he turned it. "Aw, hell!" he said aloud. "Now what the hell am I supposed to think. Damn it!"

He kept jiggling the key back and forth in the hole, turning it left and right, trying it in different positions. Nothing seemed to work. For a moment he stared at a far corner of the cabin. He was damn near better off cuffed than like this. He'd have two feet of cold steel swinging off the end of his right wrist. That ought to make for some exciting times, trying to saddle a horse or use a revolver.

He got up and went over to the fireplace. His jackknife was there. He opened it, but the blade was too thick and not sharp-pointed enough to go in the hole. He was on the point of giving up when he saw the fork

147

lying in the tin plate that Shaw had used. He picked it up. By tilting it sideways he could get two of the tines deep inside the lock. He prodded and pushed the fork into the hole, slowly working it around the circle. Nothing happened. Sometimes when he would press with the fork a certain way he'd feel something give, like it was being pushed into place. He kept up the poking and pushing, circling and circling the keyhole. All at once the cuff released. He felt the ratchet bar that encircled the bottom of his wrist come loose. He said, "Well, now I will be damned. Any prisoners I take from now on are going to eat with a spoon."

He took the manacles off his wrist, stood up, and walked over to his saddlebags. He dropped the manacles. He'd pack them later. Right then there was something he was much more interested in. He leaned down, with his hips protesting, and lifted up his saddle. His revolver lay where he'd hidden it the night before. It was the one with the six-inch barrel that he normally carried. The pistol with the nine-inch barrel had been in his saddlebags. That was the one that Jack Shaw had found and taken with him. Longarm reached down, picked up his gunbelt, and strapped it on. Then he opened the gate of the cartridge cylinder and spun it. There were five shells in the revolver, and more lying out in the desert, if he could find them. He shoved the gun into the holster. It was time to get packed up and get to making tracks. Shaw already had a three- or four-hour lead, but Longarm felt like he knew where the outlaw was headed. He might not be, but if Longarm could pick up a little sign, he felt sure he would, sooner or later, come upon the man. He wondered what Shaw had left in the corral.

It had taken him over a half an hour to get packed up, get a horse saddled, and put a second horse on lead. Every move had hurt him, and consequently, everything had seemed to take twice as long to do. He had been correct in assuming that Shaw was going to leave him the worst of the horses. Shaw had even taken the bay that Longarm had been riding. He hadn't thought so much of it the day before until Longarm had picked it out, but now he seemed to have changed his mind. The two horses he'd left were not much to begin with, and they'd been given hard usage and damn little feed. Long-arm couldn't do anything about the feed for the time being. They'd just have to travel like they had full bellies. At least they'd been well watered the last few days.

So far as food went, the horses weren't the only ones getting shorted. Shaw had not left Longarm so much as a can of tomatoes. He'd also taken a bottle of Longarm's precious Maryland whiskey. Longarm was left with barely half a quart. But that was all right. If matters went as he hoped, he expected to be in a town the following night. Once back to civilization, he could get fresh ammunition and some food and feed for the horses.

One thing that had surprised him was that he'd had two hundred dollars in folding money in his saddlebags, stuffed into the pocket of a clean shirt. Either Shaw had missed it or it was too little for him to bother with. The man, Longarm thought, was a robber but not a thief. That was a fine situation for you.

By two o'clock the prairie felt like a furnace, and he didn't reckon he'd covered half the distance to the original line cabin. Shaw had gone to no trouble to try and hide his sign, even if he could have in the loose dirt of the country. The tracks of three horses were as plain as day. A half an hour after he'd last looked at his watch, he found an empty tomato can where Shaw had obviously dropped it. The man had just punched a hole in it with his knife and then sucked all the juice out of it.

Longarm felt sure that Shaw was heading for the line cabin. That, Longarm knew, was where the money had been hidden. He didn't for a second believe that nonsense about some canyon. There was probably a canyon, all right, but it was a very small one that Shaw had dug somewhere around the cabin, though where that was, Longarm had no idea. If he succeeded in catching Shaw, the first thing he was going to ask him was where he'd hidden the money. If he wouldn't tell, Longarm was going to try and beat it out of him, and failing that, offer to let him go in exchange for the truth. Things like that ate at Longarm's vitals. He couldn't stand to be fooled like that. He'd known the day before that the money was at the cabin, but he just couldn't figure out where. It hadn't made any sense that Shaw would have hidden that amount of cash up in the mountains somewhere. Too many things could happen to it. Hell, squirrels could come along and chew it up to make a nest. Anybody could accidentally find it. No, you didn't rob that much money and then walk away without having it near your side.

It was a long day. Longarm had plenty of water out of the canvas bag Shaw had left for him, but nothing besides that except half a cigar, and water and cigar smoke weren't all that filling. The horses were looking gaunt, and there was no reason for them not to be. Being an outlaw's mount was not a good job in the general scheme of horse business. There were better jobs, like working as a carriage horse for a banker, or maybe being a lady's pleasure horse and working every other Sunday. There was the hardship of the sidesaddle, but ladies didn't weigh very much and you had plenty of time to stand around in the pasture and eat and get your strength up.

Longarm did not ordinarily dwell on such matters as what job was best for a horse. He figured maybe the sun was getting to him. But then, anything was better than thinking about the report he'd have to write if he didn't recapture Shaw. As it was, he'd been on sticky ground about transporting a prisoner from one territory to another, but that part could be made understandable with the culprit in hand and given the circumstances. But if he lost both the prisoner and the stolen money, it was going to put a far different perspective on the situation. And he wasn't just talking about handing Billy Vail a good laugh for his mistakes. This was serious business and might well lead to a reprimand or worse. Anyway you looked at it, it wasn't going to look good on either his record or his reputation. There'd be no excuses either. He'd had the prisoner in hand. His only job, besides recovering the money, had been to get Shaw behind bars. He'd failed at that. Shaw had outsmarted him, and that was a matter no lawman could have against him.

He had the faint hope that Shaw really had hidden the stolen money in a canyon in the last foothills he'd traveled through before reaching the high prairie. If that was the case, Longarm would be in an ideal spot to cut the outlaw off after he had retrieved the money and turned south again toward Mexico. But it was becoming clearer and clearer, as the day wore out and the tracks of the three horses headed relentlessly west, that Shaw was heading for the cabin. Had he been going north toward his canyon, he would have bent off to the right some time back.

It got hotter. Longarm had planned to ride one horse half of the distance and then switch. But he had further decided, at the pace he was making, that he'd wait and ride the other animal the next day. They were both about equal, with nothing outstanding to choose between them. The horse he was on was a little bigger, but he was also a little fatter than the tough-looking pony that Longarm had on a lead rope. But not fat enough. The lard was rapidly melting off him under the desert sun. The horse had been standing in somebody's barn or feed lot for too long. He was soft and not used to such work. Longarm was taking it espeically slow because he couldn't afford to have the horse quit on him. The only thing worse than having two such horses in such country was having only one.

By his watch it was closing on four o'clock when he sighted the cabin. He didn't have to look for it. If he'd kept his head down and done nothing more than watch the tracks of Shaw's horses, he would have run right into the thing. As best he could figure, he was about three or four hours behind Shaw, maybe more. But he had no intention of setting in to chase the outlaw. For one thing, the horses wouldn't have lasted, and for another, he was pretty sure he knew where Shaw was heading. After the horses had rested and drunk some water, he'd reconnoiter. He felt sure he'd find Shaw heading in exactly the direction he expected him to be.

There was a dead horse in the corral behind the cabin. It was the muscled-up dun that Shaw had been riding. There wasn't a mark on him. It was clear he had just gone sour from the work and the pace Shaw had set. Probably Shaw had let all three of his hot, worn-out horses drink their fill at the barrel, and the horse least likely to stand it had foundered and rolled over and died.

The reason Shaw hadn't waited and let his animals cool out before allowing them to drink was quickly clear to Longarm's eyes. What he saw made him want to jump up and down and gnash his teeth and bang his head against the stone wall of the cabin.

The big five-foot-high barrel was lying on its side. Longarm could see several bullet holes through it about midway up. Apparently the barrel had been too heavy to tip over when it was brimful of water, so Shaw had drained it by knocking some holes in it with .44 slugs. Longarm stood on the wet, muddy ground and shook his head, cursing himself. The money, mostly gold, had been at the bottom of the barrel. Hell, he'd drunk from the pipe coming from the windmill that had flowed into the barrel. Now, with the barrel on its side, the water was spilling out of the pipe in a thin stream onto the ground. Longarm righted the barrel and looked down to its bottom. No doubt Shaw had had some kind of oilskin covering he could wrap the money in, maybe his slicker. But it really didn't make much difference. It wasn't going to hurt the gold at all, and all it would do to paper currency was get it wet, even if Shaw had just dropped it into the barrel in the original canvas bags it had come in.

Longarm shook his head. His horses were standing outside the corral, nickering to get in and get at the water. He moved the big barrel back under the stream. It wouldn't fill back up again because of the holes halfway up its sides, but it didn't matter. The water would be close to three feet deep, and that would be plenty good enough for his horses.

While he waited for the barrel to fill, Longarm took a walk south of the cabin, cutting a wide circle. The first set of tracks he came across were headed due south. But there were way too many of them, at least twelve to fifteen horses as near as he could figure. That, of course, would be the Arizona Rangers heading dead straight for the border just as Shaw had predicted they would. Still on foot, he completed his circuit around the cabin, and was surprised to find no more tracks leaving, not in any direction. It puzzled him for a time, but then he smiled to himself and went to see to watering his horses.

It was dark by half past six. Longarm had spent the last half hour of light tearing what wood he could off the fence. Since it was all board, he was able to get a surprising amount of wood and still leave the fence intact. Shaw had, either on purpose or through forgetfulness, left Longarm's coffee intact. Even the sugar was still there, though the little bag was almost empty. He figured to have a pot of coffee before supper and then one afterwards. For supper he would smoke a cigar. But he had a more pressing need for the coffee than just for himself. Just before he went to bed he would brew up a pot, making it very strong. The next morning he would give it to both of his horses. Coffee sometimes gave him an extra burst of energy, and it would do the same for his horses. He had used the trick many times in the past and it had always worked, though it was dangerous because it caused a worn-out horse to do more than he naturally would. You didn't want to do it to the same horse very often, and you didn't want to do it to a valuable animal because it could cause a mount to not give you the clues he normally would when he was playing out. The first you'd know about it was when your horse was keeling over. Longarm's two dead horses were still where they'd fallen, except the buzzards had been at them, as well as coyotes, and they were pretty well stripped down.

That night, a little before eight, he built up a fire, made a pot of coffee, ant then sat in front of the blaze drinking coffee and whiskey and smoking a cigar.

After his horses had watered, he saddled the horse he'd ridden that day, a roan, and rode out in a line parallel to the Arizona Rangers' tracks. He rode on the eastern side of the chewed-up ground. Sure enough, as he had thought, he had not gone more than a mile when he found a set of tracks, what appeared to be two horses with one bearing more of a load than the other, branching off to the southeast. It made Longarm smile. It was such a simple trick he was amazed that Shaw would even bother with it. But then, he must have figured it would take such a little effort that it was worth doing. When Shaw had left the cabin, sometime earlier that day after he'd retrieved his money, he had disguised his direction by riding over the tracks of the posse, going far enough to hide his real intentions, but not so far as to cause himself any real inconvenience. It only served to confirm to Longarm what he'd already been thinking, what Shaw's final destination was. Looking at the tracks, Longarm knew, with a sense of satisfaction, that he and the outlaw were going to meet again and in the not-too-distant future.

Back at the cabin he sat, smoking and thinking and staring into the fire. It went back to when he and Shaw had met up by accident in Durango, when Longarm was taking some leave and had gone down to kick up his heels. They had been in a whorehouse discussing the relative merits of the Mexican *putas*. Shaw had said he didn't know why he bothered with such as he had two girls that he kept at his ranch that would put anything they had seen to shame. Longarm had been amazed. He'd said, "Ranch? Ranch? You got a ranch, Jack? I got a hard time seeing you messing with cattle. Or even raising horses. I'd guess you to be too busy on the owl-hoot trail to take time for such."

Shaw had laughed and admitted that he really wasn't much of a rancher. He'd said, "I guess it is kind of stretching it for me to call the place a ranch, since I don't keep no cattle and shore as hell don't raise no horses. Too easy to steal." He'd said that what animals were on the place belonged to the Mexicans he kept there to look after things. He'd said, "Mostly what I like about it is it's on the flat-ass prairie and you can see anybody coming for miles. I don't like being snuck up on if you take my meaning."

He had not identified the whereabouts of the ranch, but he had made several references to a town called Douglas. The only Douglas that Longarm knew about was in the extreme southeastern corner of the Arizona Territory, very close to the New Mexico line and right on the border with Mexico. The Mexican town across from Douglas was Aqua Prieta, and Shaw had mentioned it several times, mostly complaining about the lack of trade goods in the primitive place and the necessity of crossing into Arizona if you wanted to find good whiskey or cigars or cartridges. Longarm was satisfied that Shaw lived on a hacienda someplace outside of Aqua Prieta. If he did, Longarm was sure to the point of certainty that he could locate the ranch.

But that, of course, was only half the battle. The other half would be taking Shaw in, and that was no small chore. Jack Shaw, as far as Longarm was concerned, was no ordinary outlaw. Fortunately. If they were all as smart as Shaw, he reflected, his job would be a good deal harder.

As the night came on, so did the cold. Looking up at the sky, Longarm noticed that the moon was definitely on the wane. Outside, there was much less light than there had been. It was coming on to the phase of the moon that Shaw had been waiting for. Longarm calculated it to be at least a two-day ride to Douglas, and that on good horses. Probably, Longarm thought, Shaw had been able to make fifteen or twenty miles after picking up the money sometime that morning. He'd be camped somewhere along the route to Benson, which was directly on the way to Douglas and Aqua Prieta. If Shaw pushed it, the next day he could be camping close enough to the border to cross over in the dark the following morning. Longarm knew he had no hope of catching the man. He only wanted to stay close enough behind him to take him while he was at his ranch relaxing with his two women after the labors of the trail. Longarm knew he could not push the two horses. Neither one of them could take it. He had some hopes of buying another when he reached Benson, which he calculated was twenty-five miles away. He hoped to buy a good horse, but since the money would be coming out of his pocket, he had to be able to buy a horse for a good enough price that he could hope to trade it or sell it later.

Which was one irritating feature about his job. Since a federal marshal could requisition a horse or horses from any federal installation, including the cavalry, the government took the position that any horses a marshal might be forced to buy on his own were *his* problem. It was all well and good to say you could recquisition horses, but when you were in the middle of a place where there weren't any government installations and you needed a horse, what in hell were you supposed to do? Billy Vail had said that that came under the heading of the fourteenth paragraph of the federal marshals' directive, which said that a marshal should be resourceful and conserving of government property and expense. That a marshal should use his intelligence in all cases that proved to be the exception to ordinary situations, and take prudent actions to bring matters back to where they could be managed by approved and regulated methods. Longarm had wanted to know what in hell that meant. Billy Vail had said, "It means you ain't supposed to let yourself get afoot unless you are near a government facility where you can get a remount." Longarm had still wanted to know what you were supposed to do if you were afoot and there was no government facility available. Billy Vail had growled and said, "Then you better be a helluva horse trader or you are gonna be money out of pocket."

It made Longarm smile to himself. He wished to hell he was back in Denver, sitting with Billy, eating a big steak and perhaps looking forward to a visit that night with that lady who ran the dress shop. Now *she* was a woman he could have used to distract himself the night he was lying in the little wash. But he stopped himself. He still had too much trail left before he could let himself start thinking like that.

He was hungry that night. He calculated he'd eaten exactly two meals in the past three or four days, and neither of them had been much to get excited about. Outside, in the corral, the horses nickered occasionally. He knew they weren't calling to other horses; probably asking where the groceries were. Longarm wondered the same thing himself. He'd made his bed in front of the fireplace, and it was still burning enough to throw rosy glows against the walls of the cabin. Longarm had set his mind to wake up in about four or five hours. Since he knew where he was headed, he could travel in the dark. It would be a lot easier on the horses. With any luck he could reach Benson and get them some feed not too long after daylight.

Chapter 10

In the end he had to feed the coffee to the horses out of his hat. It didn't much matter since the hat was pretty well gone anyway. But it did irritate him that he'd have to spend a few minutes and use one of his shirts to wipe the thing out after the horses got through drooling and slopping around inside the crown.

Fortunately, both horses liked the coffee. He gave them each about a quart. By the time he was ready to break trail, they both seemed to have a good deal more energy. As he was saddling up he had to smile, remembering the young deputy marshal he'd told about the coffee trick. The young man had come back to him a few weeks later as reproachful as a Sunday School teacher. He'd told Longarm that just because he was young and inexperienced wasn't any reason to play such a mean prank on him. Longarm had been puzzled until the young deputy had said, "Hell, Longarm, that damn horse spit and spewed coffee all over me. Like to have burned a brand-new five-dollar shirt off my back, to say nothin' of what it done to my bare skin." Longarm had stared at him a long time, too dumbfounded to say a word. He could not believe that the young man had tried to give hot coffee to his horse. When he'd finally asked about it, the young deputy had said, "Why, hell, yes.

That's the way I take it. What'd you want me to do, saucer and blow it fer him?''

As Longarm finally set out, both horses were feeling lively from the cold night weather. He figured they'd have different thoughts once the sun began its work. He'd saddled the smaller horse, a black with two white stocking feet. It was not quite four o'clock when he got them headed toward the southwest, steering by different stars he knew but didn't know the names of. The only one he could ever recall was the North Star.

By the time dawn arrived, he didn't know how far they'd come—maybe ten miles—but the little black was surprising him by his endurance. He'd expected the horse to play out fairly quickly, but the animal moved right along. Still, to be certain and to play it safe, he switched horses about seven o'clock and rode the roan the rest of the way into Benson.

It was a slow trip. It took them six hours to make what he guessed was about twenty-five miles. Still, he arrived with both horses.

Benson was an ugly little weatherbeaten town with a population of around two thousand and five times as many saloons as churches. Half the town appeared to be Mexican, and there was only one discernible street, though there were wagon-track trails leading off in every direction. The downtown buildings were mostly frame, looking worn and colorless as a result of the sun and the sand and the wind. Longarm had been conscious that the land was descending gradually all the way from the line cabin. By the time he reached the border at Douglas, it should have dropped two or three thousand feet in elevation. It made for easier breathing by both man and beast.

He rode into the town on the main street, noting with satisfaction that they had at least two cafes. There was also a ramshackle hotel and a few boardinghouses and, he was glad to see, a livery stable. Most of the residences, either in town or on the outskirts, looked to be adobe, with only the bigger ones being constructed of

159

lumber or brick. He turned in at the livery stable and had both horses seen to. He was desperate to get himself to a cafe and get some food in his own belly, but he stayed at the stable and supervised the graining of his horses. He wanted to make sure the horses got their fill, but he didn't want them eating too much at one time. Even though he was into Benson early enough to rest up and then push on, he saw no real reason for hurry. Shaw was where he was going if that was where he was going. Hurry now was pointless. He and the horses could both use a rest before he pushed on for the last fifty miles to Douglas. He had harbored some hope that there was a railroad line to Douglas, but that was not the case. There was an east-west track through town, but not one running north-south. A train went west to Tucson and east into New Mexico, but nothing was going where he wanted to go.

When he was satisfied his horses had been attended to, he took himself down to the nearest cafe and ordered steak and eggs. The steak was stringy and tough, and the eggs weren't cooked the way he liked them, with the yokes liquid, but he cleaned his plate and then ordered the same thing again. While he waited, he ate a half a dozen biscuits with butter and honey and drank three cups of coffee, putting as much sugar in it as he liked.

Finally, feeling as if he had regained some lost ground, he left the cafe and went looking for the sheriff's office. The sheriff, an older, grizzled man with a drooping mustache, stared at him in some amazement. He said, "Marshal, do I hear you right? You are askin' me if I seen a stranger, a white man, passin' through who woulda been ridin' one horse an' leadin' a extry? That right?"

Longarm nodded.

The sheriff leaned back in his chair. "Not more'n a half a dozen. 'Less he was wearin' spangles or pink tights, I can't he'p you a bit. And no, 'bout the other question, I don't know no Jack Shaw. Heered of him,

160

but never met the sucker, I'm right glad to say.''

Longarm thanked the sheriff, and then went down and got a room at the rundown-looking hotel. He was going to have a sleep in a real bed even if it didn't amount to much more than a nap.

After that he went looking around the livery stable to see what kind of horses they had for sale. He didn't see anything that looked much better than what he had. The man at the livery stable told him there was a horse trader out a mile, but Longarm decided he'd save that for later. Right then he wanted a drink and he wanted it in a glass and in a saloon. He also wanted a couple of beers to go with it. He wanted to sit in a cool, dim saloon for about two hours and have a few quiet drinks and rest his spirit as best he could. It had been a hard assignment that had taken longer than he'd thought, and was not having anywhere near as good a result as he'd expected.

He stopped in at a general mercantile store and considered buying another rifle. In the end all he purchased was a box of cartridges for his pistol. Jack Shaw had his rifle, and he intended on getting it back. He was used to that rifle, and it was a weapon that had seen him through some tight places. He was damned if he was going to lay out forty-five dollars for another one when his was only half a hundred miles from him. Besides, he didn't think the showdown with Shaw was going to take place at long range. He wanted the man alive, and that didn't call for rifle work. What he wanted the most was to get close enough to get his hands on Shaw. The man had caused him considerable trouble, and he had every intention of beating the billy blue hell out of him.

Longarm went to bed at about two o'clock in the afternoon, and slept until eight that night. He got up and ate a big supper at the same cafe, and then came back and went to sleep again, and slept until a little after one in the morning. Sitting, yawning, and still groggy, he forced himself to his feet and went sleepily down to the livery stable, his saddlebags over his shoulder. He woke the night man, who helped him rig up, and then was on his way by two o'clock in the morning. He would have at least five hours of cool traveling during the night before the blazing sun got up enough to do real damage.

Fortunately, there was a stage and wagon road to Douglas, so he didn't have to go cross-country over the rough, barren terrain which seemed capable only of supporting sand and rocks and where every growing thing seemed compelled to armor itself in stickers or thorns.

He was riding the roan and leading the little black. He had not been satisfied with any trade he could make, either with the quality of the horseflesh or the price of the animal. In the end he'd decided to try to make it on the two he had left. Both seemed to have benefited by the day of rest and the feed. It wasn't as cold as it had been up on the high prairie. Still, Longarm could see his breath and the breath of the horses as he left the dark town behind and set out on his trip. He figured to travel for six hours and then look for a place to lay up during the hottest part of the day. After that, if the horses were up to it, he intended to push on for Douglas, hoping to arrive sometime in the early night hours. The biggest problem was that there was no water on the way. He was carrying enough for himself, of course, but the horses would have to make it through again dry. As weakened as they were, it was not a situation he much relished. The livery man had said he might get lucky and run across a freighter who'd have a barrel of water for his own stock and who might let Longarm refresh his stock for a price. Other than that, he'd found no way to carry water that wouldn't defeat its own purpose by being more of a load than it was worth. Most riders heading to Douglas were riding fresh, rested, and well-fed animals who were strong enough for the task, and the travelers pushed straight on through, making the fifty-mile jump in one stretch. And a man could do that if he had a horse capable of sustaining seven or eight miles an hour, but Longarm was afraid to push his mounts at a pace much faster than a man could walk.

162

At least there was the road. As the moon commenced to get down and it got darker and darker, Longarm was more and more grateful for the rough but recognizable road. He would have hated to be traveling without one across such rough country in such darkness. It was a quick way to break a horse's leg.

He had restocked his whiskey and cigars, and as he rode along he would, from time to time, turn in the saddle and fetch out a bottle of whiskey. Of course he hadn't been able to find any of his Maryland whiskey in such an outpost as Benson, but the popskull he'd obtained would make you just as drunk and leave you with just as bad a head the next morning. But he was drinking purely for medicinal purposes, to ward off the cold.

As he rode, he deliberately did not let himself dwell on Jack Shaw, or try and imagine what the situation might be that he would have to face when he finally ran the man to ground. He'd learned the hard way not to scale mountains or swim rivers until you got to them. You could visualize what a situation was going to be, make plans to overcome it, and then find out all your imagination had been for naught when you finally got to the scene and found it was nothing like you'd expected. He'd just handle the situation, whatever it might be, when he got to it.

Dawn took a long time to arrive, and Longarm was thourghly tired of the unchanging dark as they plodded through it. He wondered if Shaw was using the night cover to cross over from the U.S. to his ranch in Mexico. Maybe he'd already made the crossing. Longarm didn't know and didn't care. All of that could wait until they met. At least now, he wouldn't be burdened by trying to find out where Shaw had hidden the money. But in many ways, he wished he hadn't found out. It made him feel like a damn fool. He remembered with a twinge how Shaw had been so eager to fill the water bags from the pipe and fill the coffeepot. He hadn't wanted Longarm anywhere near that barrel. And yet Longarm had drunk from that pipe, but he'd never thought to poke around in the dark water of the barrel. Well, it was all just as well. Longarm had been needing a good bringing down for some time, and Shaw was doing a good job of handling the task.

Finally it was good daylight. The road ahead and behind was empty. Longarm would have to wait for several hours if he was to have any hope of meeting a wagoneer who might have extra water to sell. He could see, by looking behind him, that the terrain was continuing to slope downwards the further south he went. It was ugly, bleak country, even less inviting than the high prairie, which at least grew greasewood and bunchgrass. Nothing appeared to grow in this desolate country except snakes and sagebrush and spiders and cactus. Off to his left he could see a small range of mountains, but he knew the jagged crests were at least fifty miles away, if not further. He figured they were probably part of the Sierra Madre range in northern Mexico.

It got to be eight in the morning. Since the sun had been up good, Longarm had begun looking around for someplace to shelter during the heat of the day. The only thing he'd seen had been some cactus about four feet tall. There was no sign of a tree, much less a grove of trees. Naturally, there was no sign of any kind of building. Why would anyone build a dwelling or a barn or any other sort of structure in such a place? You couldn't grow a crop in such a place, so you didn't need a farmhouse. And you damn sure couldn't raise cattle or horses or even goats, so you didn't need a ranch headquarters. He'd been an idiot to have expected to find shelter in such a terrain and country. He should have let the horses rest all night and started about noon. That way they would have only gotten six or seven hours of the worst of the sun and he could have pushed on at night. But it was too late for such thinking.

He kept on until nine and then ten, going slower and slower. He could tell by the saliva flecking around the bit of the roan that the horse badly needed water. Dry spit was a bad sign in a horse.

An hour later, with no sign of shelter and no sign of a wagon, either coming or going, Longarm had about reached the decision to stop and rest the horses, shade or no shade, when he felt the first tremor between his legs. He did not hesitate. He immediately pulled the roan to a halt and leapt to the ground. But even in that short a time the horse was already beginning to shake all over. Longarm had seen it before, and it was a sight he hated. As quickly as he could, he undid the saddle cinch and let it swing free below the horse's belly. By now the horse had spraddled out his legs in an effort to stay erect. Longarm took his pocketknife out and opened it. He felt for the vein at the front of the horse's neck, and then made a quick slash with his knife. He had tried it only once before and it hadn't worked then, but he was willing to make any effort because, if he didn't, the outcome was a foregone conclusion. The theory was that opening a vein and allowing the horse to bleed a little cooled the animal down. At least that was what the old-timers said. He stood back, watching the blood running down the animal's neck and dripping on the ground. The smell frightened the black, and he started running back and forth at the end of his lead rope, neighing uncertainly.

Longarm watched. For a second he thought the roan might be getting better, but then the horse started staggering sideways—the blind staggers, they called it—and then he seemed to sigh and sink down by the hindquarters. Before it could get caught under the collapsing horse, Longarm reached out, grabbed his saddle, and jerked it off the animal's back. He stepped aside as the horse slowly crumpled to the ground, landing on his belly as Longarm's foundered animal had. He didn't stay backside-up long. Little by little he leaned over until he toppled onto his left side. He twitched once, and then was still.

Longarm cursed. He cursed for two or three minutes straight. He'd ridden other horses to death, and would probably ride others to death in the future, but he'd always hated it and would continue to hate it even though, in all cases, he'd never really had much choice. This horse had been misused, by himself and by others before him. The poor animal had never had a chance to recover from the nearly two weeks of bad treatment and hard usage he'd undergone. It was criminal to take horses into country where they couldn't get feed and water, but unfortunately, the men Longarm was usually chasing were already criminals, and a horse here or there didn't make a damn bit of difference to them.

In the end there was nothing left to do except take his bridle off the roan and put it on the black. He could see that the black had a mouth full of dry spittle also. He wouldn't last long if Longarm kept riding.

The roan had fallen off the road. As Longarm saddled the black and adjusted his saddlebags and tied them in place, he looked down at the animal. Overhead the buzzards were already starting to circle. At least the horse wouldn't be a complete waste. The buzzards and coyotes would see to that.

It made no sense to stop. It was just as hot standing as it was moving. But Longarm figured he could at least spare the black the extra effort of his weight. He took one of the two water bags he had, poured as much in his hat as he could, and let the horse drink what he could get down. It wasn't much, and he spilled as much as he drank. Longarm had about two gallons of water, and a horse could sweat five gallons in an hour, more under such a sun. A horse couldn't really carry enough water on his back to satisfy his own needs. It was an odd thing to think about, but it was true. Longarm had seen the proof of it many times.

It was warm work, walking down the uneven road in his high-heeled boots. But there was no help for it. The next time he lost a horse he would be afoot. Even not riding, he glanced back anxiously from time to time to see how the black was doing. The horse was covered with lines of dried sweat all over his glistening black hide. The glistening was caused by fresh sweat and not good health. But at least, Longarm reflected, he still had enough water in him to sweat.

Longarm didn't know how far he had walked, but he knew it was approaching one o'clock when he and the horse topped a little rise in the road and he saw, in the distance, a small line of three wagons. He stopped and shaded his eyes, peering through the shimmering heat waves. It was a long moment before he was able to discern that the wagons were heading his way. Only then did he allow himself a drink of water. Once again he filled the crown of his hat with the liquid and let the black snuffle around in it. He said to the horse, "Maybe, when them wagons get here, we can get some of this stuff in your belly."

He rode into Douglas at a little past seven o'clock. He had made the trip in one day even though it had cost him a horse. When they arrived it was difficult to say who was the most tired, Longarm or his remaining horse. He went straight to a livery stable and had the black put up in a stall with strict instructions on his watering and feeding. He wanted the horse to eat hay before he ate anything else such as grain, and he made it clear to the stable hands that he was fond of the animal and that he was a federal marshal, and that it would be in their best interests to give the animal the best care they knew how. He didn't come out and say it, but he conveyed the impression the best he could that he would arrest the lot of them if anything happened to the horse.

After that, he went down to a hotel and got a room and ordered up a bath. When it came he sat in the tub, ordering the Mexican boys who were fetching the hot water to "keep it coming and make damn sure it's hot." After he had washed for a while, he fetched a basin over to the tub and shaved while he was soaking in the hot water. The parts of him that weren't still sore from lifting the roof were tired and sore from walking the two or three miles he'd trod along in his high-heeled boots. His feet felt like they had blisters all over them, but fortunately, the unaccustomed activity hadn't gone on

167

long enough to produce any serious harm. His feet were just sore. Once he'd seen the wagons, he and the black had stood there by the side of the road and let the freighters come to them. They had had water for his horse, and had even sold him some grain mixed with shelled corn to give the animal something solid for his stomach. The feed and the water had revived the black enough so that they had stepped along and made Douglas without camping. Longarm was starting to have a real respect for the tough little animal. He hadn't looked like much, but he was proving to have a lot of bottom.

Once he'd gotten about four layers of dirt and a week's worth of whiskers off him, Longarm rustled around in his saddlebags and found a clean shirt and socks, and even a pair of jeans he'd only worn for two or three days—and that had been in town. They were nearly as good as new. After he'd changed clothes and combed his hair, despairing of his hat, he went downstairs and ate in the hotel dining room. Douglas was a border town and border towns, Longarm knew, were pretty much the same from the tip of Texas all the way up the line to California. In a border town you were neither in the United States or Mexico. You were in a border town, and there wasn't any other way to describe it.

He had beef stew and biscuits for supper that night, and he ate until he was full. After that he sought out the best of the saloons, and drank some brandy and played a little poker. He'd put his badge in his pocket, so the other players treated him like an ordinary citizen and managed to win twenty dollars off him. He didn't much care. It was pleasant to sit and do something besides chase bandits over barren country. He had no intention of keeping on to Aqua Prieta that night, even though it was only about a half mile away. Shaw could wait. Either he'd be there the next day or he wouldn't. All Longarm knew was that he was going to sleep all night in a bed. He went down and checked on the black, and then he went to his hotel room. He'd bought a bottle of brandy, and he intended to bite off a piece of that and then wear the bed out.

The next morning he had breakfast, and then mounted the black and rode on over to Aqua Prieta. It was difficult to tell when you passed from the U.S. into Mexico since the country didn't change at all and Aqua Prieta just looked like a poor section of Douglas. The only marker was a shack with a uniformed guard slumped inside, drinking something out of a bottle. There was a post with a sign on it that said, "*Bienvenudos a Mexico*." "Welcome to Mexico." That, Longarm thought, was a laugh. The only thing welcome in Mexico was your dollars, and they'd have been just as happy if you'd mailed the money across or wrapped it around a rock and chunked it. Still, Longarm in the main liked Mexico. He liked the *peones,* the *campesinos*, the *vaqueros,* the working people of the country. He found them, even as poor as Job's turkey, to be serious, dignified, and courteous to a fault. They were a proud people, even in their poverty, and strictly honest. It was said in Mexico that you could leave a roasted pig in the middle of a plaza and unless a *rico,* a rich man, or a *politico,* which was one and the same, came by, the pig would be there the next day. Longarm had always thought it was a good story, but he'd doubted he'd much care for pig, roasted or not, after it had been sitting out in the Mexican sun for a couple of days.

Once into Aqua Prieta, he tied his horse in front of a cantina and got a beer and began in his poor Spanish, asking about the ranchero of *el pistolero gringo*. The third man he asked knew, or seemed to know, who he was talking about. The man said he was a farmer, a *campesino,* and described Jack Shaw even to the birthmark. Longarm's informant, who was a sun-dried little *peon* wearing white pants tied at the ankle and a wool *pancho* over his white shirt, said that Shaw lived on a large hacienda about two miles to the west and south of town. Longarm asked the man if he would be willing to show him to the hacienda in return for a little gift for his family, a little gift of money. You never, Longarm knew, wanted to insult a proud man, no matter how poor he was, by trying to give him money for an errand he would consider a duty and an honor to do for a stranger. It was all right, however, to offer the gift of money for his family, his wife and *niños*. That was a perfectly acceptable gesture.

The man rode a small mule without a saddle. Longarm had to slow the black to his pace. A little way out of town Longarm could see immediately what Shaw had meant about being able to spot anyone coming from a long way off. Except for groves of ash and mountain pine and mesquite that were sparsely scattered about, the land was flat and mainly uninhabited, though a few small farms were struggling to grow little patches of corn.

Longarm was almost certain he recognized Shaw's place even before the little Mexican said anything. He pulled up the black and pointed at a big adobe building at least a mile in the distance but looking closer because of the thin air. *"Es este por el señor gringo del pistoles?"* "Does this belong to the American with the pistols?"

"Sí."

"Seguro?" "For sure?"

"Sí."

Longarm dismounted and stood behind the black. He reached into his near saddlebag and took out his telescope. With the naked eye he could see a few figures moving around the hacienda, but he couldn't make out who or what they were. With the *campesino* watching him curiously, he extended the telescope and put it to his eye. The scene instantly jumped much closer. He could see that the big adobe ranch house had once been whitewashed, but sand and wind had combined to turn it into a very pale tan. It looked to be a residence of at least six rooms. Longarm was able to get a fair idea of its inside size by the number of round ceiling beams that stuck out through the outer walls. It had a roof made of

170

red clay tiles. There was a front courtyard that was bounded by a low wall. Behind the house were several small frame buildings that Longarm took to be a stable and two or three sheds that were most likely used for storage. He turned his glass one after another on the several figures. There were two behind the house, working around the sheds, and one man just outside the front of the dwelling standing in the courtyard who was cut off at the hips by the low wall. The two figures in the back were clearly Mexican laborers. As near as Longarm could see they were not wearing guns. He swung the glass around to the man in the front. As he brought the figure into focus the man turned and took a step back onto the front patio and then disappeared. Longarm had only gotten a quick look, but there was no mistaking that appearance. It was Shaw, all right. Nobody else could look quite as cocky just standing in their front yard as Jack Shaw.

Longarm closed the spyglass and put it thoughtfully back into his saddlebag. The house was going to be very difficult to approach. There were no bars on the windows, but the house was surrounded by flat, cleared land on all sides for a distance of at least two hundred yards. Anybody either trying to walk up or ride up to that house was going to be exposed for a long time and a long way. For a moment Longarm leaned his arms on the dish of his saddle and stared across the way at the hacienda. There was a small grove of mountain pine on the side toward the road, the side that Longarm was viewing the house from. The pines weren't very tall, no more than ten or twelve feet, but they were thick and the copse was a good forty yards wide. A man could ride down the road past the house and then, with the pines blocking the view from the house, make a dash into the little grove and hide. The only problem with that was that it still left you four hundred yards from the hacienda. If Shaw had a guard posted, anyone trying to slip up to the place would be spotted whether the guard was any good or not. But then, Longarm thought, why should

Shaw post a guard? He was in Mexico. He was safe. The danger was north, in Arizona Territory. He had nothing to fear from the gringo law. They couldn't operate in Mexico.

No, they couldn't. Not if they played by the rules. But then, Longarm had no intention of playing by the rules. He had just seen the man who had damaged his reputation with the Marshals Service, and he did not intend that Shaw would get away with it.

He mounted and turned his horse for Aqua Prieta. The little *campesino* was looking at him questioningly. *"Esta bueno?"*

Longarm shook his head. He said, *"Es no mi amigo. Es un otro hombre."* "It is not my friend. It is some other man."

"Aaah," the campesino said. *"Es malo suerte."*

"Sí," Longarm said in agreement. It was bad luck, but he didn't say for whom.

As they rode back Longarm studied the problem, turning it over and over in his mind. If he had any sense he'd simply set up watch on the place and bide his time until Shaw ventured out to town or someplace else. Then he'd be easy to take. Find a hiding place on his route and jump out and throw down on him.

Except Longarm wasn't in a waiting mood. He'd been on the trail too long. He'd been sleepy and thirsty and hungry for a lot longer than he cared for. Besides, there were several lady friends of his that he had been depriving too long. No, he was going to settle Jack Shaw within twenty-four hours or know the reason why.

He had, of course, lied to the *campesino* about it being the wrong man at the wrong ranch. Even though he wasn't wearing his badge, he didn't want it getting about that there was a gringo looking for the *pistolero gringo.* This way no one was the wiser. Longer gave the little Mexican a five-dollar gold piece, which made the man's eyes get big in his head. Probably it was the most money he had ever held in his hand at one time. Jack Shaw had finally been a benefactor to a community that he lived in. That five dollars would buy an awful lot of beans and tortillas and fill a lot of empty bellies. Longarm wanted to be sure and remember to tell Shaw what good works he'd caused to be done in his name. Longarm had the feeling, though, that Shaw wasn't going to be all that interested.

When they got back to town, Longarm put his horse back in the stable, and then found a sort of cafe where he had a meal of *huevos rancheros:* eggs with chili sauce and cheese. It was not eaten with a utensil but with a rolled-up flour tortilla that you used as a kind of scoop. He thought it was the best meal he'd had since he'd left Denver. After he'd eaten, he went to a kind of little inn and rented a room. He intended to sleep through the afternoon, and then arise about six and go to making his preparations for that night.

Chapter 11

In the evening he bought a striped, many-colored wool *poncho* that would go over his head and hang off his shoulders nearly to his knees. It was too heavy to wear during the day, although he saw plenty of the Mexicans wearing *ponchos,* but it would be welcome during the long, cold night. He also bought a very wide-brimmed straw sombrero with a conical crown. The sombrero was not for comfort but for deception. He also went to the livery stable and arranged to rent a mule along with one of the uncomfortable wooden saddles that they used.

When it was about eight o'clock, he went back to the little cafe and had some beans, rice, and corn tortillas and drank some more of the green beer. It was so bad he finally decided that the fault must lie with him. No one could make something that bad and expect the public to buy it. He'd heard of "shotgun whiskey," moonshine that was so bad you had to hire a man to hold a shotgun on you to force you to drink it, but the only thing to recommend the beer was how cheap it was, about a penny a glass. Still, even at that price, Longarm didn't think it was much of a bargain.

He was diverting himself with different thoughts, a method he often used to keep himself from getting worked up too soon about a particularly important piece of business.

After supper he strolled around in the night air, wearing his *poncho,* taking in the sights of the town. Except for one cantina where it sounded as if things were getting pretty lively, the town was dead quiet. There was an establishment that Longarm felt pretty sure was a whorehouse. He gave it some thought, but decided that it might take a little of his edge off and he figured to need all the alertness he could get. At about ten o'clock he went to the little inn and turned in fully clothed. He knew, with the nap he'd taken that afternoon, that he was not likely to sleep more than four or five hours.

It was about four in the morning when he went down to the livery and got the mule, already saddled and bridled. He gave the night boy five pesos to thank him for his trouble, and then swung into the wooden saddle. The thing was as uncomfortable as it looked. It had been made for someone about half his size and weight. The mule turned out to be a tough, cold-jawed little brute who did not want to do night work. Longarm had to battle him around the town a couple of circuits before the mule finally got it into his head that only one of them was going to decide which direction they went and when.

When he finally had the mule lined out, Longarm started them south for the edge of town and the fork in the road that ran west and would take him by Shaw's place. It was a very dark night, one that Longarm thought that Shaw would have appreciated. He reckoned it to be not much more than an hour before dawn. He calculated he wouldn't have too long a wait.

They reached the fork in the road, and Longarm turned the mule west. He was riding with his legs hanging down, not using the stirrups. He had his straw sombrero on, tilted forward as he had seen the Mexicans wear theirs. He was wearing his *poncho,* and he

175

was riding slumped in the saddle to minimize his size. Of course a close observer would have seen his high-heeled boots and figured him not to be a Mexican, but he didn't think there were any close observers out that night. All he wanted to do was blend in as best he could with the country, not cause any notice to anyone who might have been up at that hour.

In the darkness ahead he could see the grove of pines. It was about forty or fifty yards off the road, on the left. Longarm aimed the mule slightly off the road, heading toward the edge of the copse. As he came near it, as it slowly grew in size and began to block out the hacienda, Longarm slowly pulled the mule up. The pine grove was about ten yards to his left. He was hidden from view by the trees. He raised his right leg over the mule's neck and vaulted out of the saddle and to the ground. The mule paused, but Longarm gave him a slap on the rump and the animal started and went off, switching his tail, making it plain he was irritated. He was a stable mule, spoiled like stable horses. Longarm watched while the mule went on down the road a few hundred yards. Then, as if he'd suddenly realized he wasn't being ridden any longer, the mule stopped. He looked over his shoulder. He didn't know what had happened, but he knew it was to his advantage. Longarm saw the mule turn and then head back down the road at a trot. He was heading back to his stable, the warm place where they kept the hay and the feed. Longarm watched until the mule disappeared into the darkness, and then carefully entered the grove.

He squatted at the south side of the copse, carefully watching the ranch house and waiting for signs of light. He had not wanted to keep the mule with him in the trees for fear the animal might start calling to horses at Shaw's place. Mules were a good deal smarter than horses, and demons for causing trouble when none was called for. He'd been pretty certain that the mule would head back to the stable, but it hadn't much mattered to him if it did or not. So far as getting back to town was concerned, Longarm figured that Jack Shaw would lend him a horse. Either that or he wasn't going to need one. Longarm had no illusions that Shaw would be an easy target. But he was determined that the man was going to be his prisoner or a corpse in a short while. He did not intend to give Shaw any sort of a chance. Ideally, he would like to catch Shaw as Shaw had him, in bed and asleep. But he doubted that would be the case. Longarm didn't want to work in the dark in strange country, and he expected that once the sun was up, Shaw would be too.

He could see that there were three windows on the side of the house facing his way. He intended to head for a space between the second and third window. More than likely, if Shaw slept on that side of the house, his bedroom would be in the back.

It was cold. Longarm had his arms huddled inside the *poncho,* hugging himself. He had his revolver stuck down in his waistband, not wanting to wear his gunbelt. You didn't often see a *campesino* wearing a gunbelt, much less boots, and that was what Longarm was trying to pass as, at least in a bad light.

And then he saw a little flush of pink begin in the eastern sky. He didn't hesitate. In one motion he was on his feet and moving toward he house. He kept his arms inside the *poncho,* his right hand on the butt of his revolver. He walked unsteadily, which was not difficult in high-heeled boots over the rough ground, trying to give the impression of a drunk just staggering home.

From under the brim of the big sombrero he saw the base of the house loom up. He lifted his head just enough to make sure of his direction, and staggered on. Within a few steps he was at the side of Shaw's ranch house. He dropped down, closer to the third window than the second. He hoped they would light candles or kerosene lamps inside. It would be a sign to him that people were up and moving around. He doubted he'd be able to hear through the thick walls if they just started talking to each other.

As the sun began to get up and light slowly drove off the last gray of dawn, he looked down the line at the outbuildings. What he'd taken for a stable was obviously a bunkhouse of some kind because it had a chimney sticking up and, even as Longarm watched, a thin wisp of smoke began to rise. There was no one moving around, at least not yet, but he knew it was only a matter of moments and he knew how exposed he was. He was taking a terrible gamble that the men on Shaw's place were just *peones* and not *pistoleros*. But then, he couldn't see what Shaw would want with Mexican gunmen. Mexico was his refuge, his hideout. He wouldn't need men on the place to protect it and him.

To his right he saw a glow from the second window. He was on the point of crawling that way when he heard a voice to his right, from the third window. He turned back. Almost as he did, a light began casting shadows through the window on the ground. He turned back and inched his way up to the window, taking off his hat as he did. He edged an eye over the window sill and looked in. The room was alight with rays from a kerosene lantern. As he got a view of the room he saw that it was a bedroom, and then he saw the bed, and then he saw Shaw sitting up in the bed. Shaw had his legs under the covers, but Longarm could see that he was wearing the bottoms of a set of long underwear. He was bare-chested. Longarm could see that the outlaw was talking to someone across the room out of view of the window. Then, as Longarm looked, a beautiful naked Mexican girl came into his line of sight. She walked to the edge of Shaw's bed, put her hand on the foot-post of the bed, and listened to something Shaw was saying. Longarm judged her to be about twenty or twenty-one, and he could see that Shaw hadn't lied about her looks if she was one of the two he'd been talking about.

But he had no time to look at the girl. He suddenly realized he couldn't let her get any closer to Shaw. If she got in bed with him or sat down beside him, she'd interfere with his field of fire. He knew he was going to have to act immediately. There were no curtains on the window, and for that Longarm was thankful. The window was split into four panes, separated by pieces of wood. Longarm didn't hesitate. He drew back his arm and smashed out the bottom two panes with his pistol. As quick as he could he shoved his hand and arm into the room, cocking the hammer of his revolver. He yelled, "Shaw! Freeze! Don't move, dammit!"

He saw Shaw react instantly, sliding sideways off the bed and disappearing out of sight. The girl had looked Longarm's way, and was staring at him with big, dark, luminous eyes. He yelled again. "Shaw! Give up!"

Just beyond the girl he could see another window on the other side of the room. At the instant he was expecting Shaw to come up from beside the bed with a gun in his hand, the outlaw came up behind the girl. Longarm searched for a shot. He yelled, "Shaw, give up, dammit! You can't get out!"

Then he heard the sound of glass breaking and saw legs and feet as Shaw dove through the broken window. Longarm got up, cursing, and ran to the end of the house. He didn't know if Shaw had armed himself or not. He hesitate for a second, and then peered around the back corner of the house. He saw Shaw suddenly come running out through some door or gate at the back of a kind of courtyard. Longarm yelled, "Shaw!" He stepped out into the open. But before he could fire, Shaw suddenly jerked open the door to a small shed and jumped inside. Longarm had not seen a gun in his hand, but he'd had only a fraction of a second before Shaw had disappeared. Crouched, his gun forward and still cocked, Longarm advanced toward the little shed. He figured for certain that Shaw must have gone in the hut to get a gun of some kind. He wished there was more shelter. Out of the corner of his right eye he saw a face and head poke out the door of what he'd decided was someone's living quarters or a bunkhouse of some kind. He turned his revolver in that direction and the head disappeared.

He stopped about five yards short of the shed. He crouched down and said, "Jack, you are in there and I know it. I can see all around that little chicken coop. Now you come out or I am gonna go to testing that wood you are hiding behind and see how thick it is. I don't think it will stop a bullet, Jack."

For a moment he didn't think he was going to get a response, but then Shaw said, "Longarm? What in hell are you doing here? This is Mexico!"

"I know that, Jack. I came to get you. Figured you got lost somehow."

Shaw's voice was bewildered. "You can't take me, Longarm. This is Mexico. What the hell is the matter with you?"

"I know it's Mexico, Jack. And you know it is. And you can complain to the authorities when I take you back to Arizona. They might turn you loose."

There was a half a moment of silence. Shaw said finally, "Aw, hell, Longarm, why don't you forget about me. Let it go."

"You know that ain't gonna happen, Jack. And this time I'm going to have to get the money and take it back."

Shaw laughed. "That's still got your back up, don't it, Custis. That I lied to you about the money."

"Jack, you better come on out. One of these Mexicans is liable to get brave and you wouldn't want that on your conscience."

"According to you I ain't got one. What you got in mind, Longarm?"

"I got Arizona in mind."

"I thought we was going to New Mexico."

180

"I done tried that. You didn't want to go to New Mexico. You run off."

There was a silence. "Longarm, they liable to hang me in Arizona."

"That ain't none of my affair, Jack. Like I say, I just catch 'em."

"I hear they tie your hands behind your back when they hang you. I couldn't stand that."

Longarm said, "I understand you ain't got long to worry about it, Jack. Now listen, I'm getting worried about you out in this cold with nothing on but the bottoms to your long handles. I reckon I'm going to have to test those walls, Jack." He got up and eased around to his left so he could see what was behind the shed. There was nothing. He took a few steps to his right. The shed was a dead end if you were inside.

Shaw said, "I hear they hold you pretty tight when you are waiting to be hung. I hear they pen you up pretty good in a tight little cell."

"You ought not to pay so much attention to what you hear, Jack. You coming out or not?"

There was a pause. "No deal on New Mexico, Longarm? It ain't ten miles to the territory line."

"Not again, Jack. Naw, I reckon it'll have to be Arizona."

Shaw laughed. "I don't reckon you'd put them same manacles back on me, would you, Custis?"

"Never can tell. Got about another half minute, Jack. I'm getting nervous."

A few beats passed, and then the door of the shed flew open and Jack Shaw came charging straight for Longarm. He had something black in his right hand. Longarm yelled, "Stop! Hands up!"

Shaw did not pause. He kept coming. In an instant he was within two strides of Longarm. Almost sorrowfully, Longarm aimed and pulled the trigger. His revolver boomed and Shaw stopped as if grabbed by a giant hand and then went backwards; he staggered and then fell on his back.

Longarm walked cautiously to his side, cocking his revolver as he did. Shaw looked up. There was a slight grin on his face. He lifted his right hand. He was holding a piece of kindling wood, blackened from a fire. Shaw said, as the stick fell out of his hand, "Fooled you, Custis. Made you shoot."

Longarm knelt by him. There was a hole on the right side of his chest. Little bubbles of pink froth churned around it. He was lung-shot. Longarm grimaced. He said, "I thought you said you wouldn't do it this way, Jack. When I was telling you about it, you said it wasn't for you."

Shaw coughed. He said, his voice growing faint and hoarse, "Wasn't no guilt involved, Custis. Want you to un'nerstan' that. No guilt. Couldn't take the idea of bein' pent up, Custis. Un'erstan'?"

"I guess so, Jack."

"Ain't 'bout guilt or no guilty conscience."

"If you say so, Jack."

"You'd of had to bound my hands 'hind my back, Custis. Wouldn't you?"

Shaw's voice was getting weaker and he was starting to slur his words. Longarm said, "I reckon so, Jack."

Shaw grinned. He said faintly, "I fooled you, Custis." He opened his mouth to say something else; instead he coughed up a great gout of blood. His body suddenly jerked and heaved. His eyes glazed over. He opened his mouth again and then shut it. His body settled back. Longarm reached over and closed his eyes. Then he stood up. As he turned toward the house he saw the two Mexican women standing there. They had wrapped themselves in blankets. Their eyes followed Longarm as he walked past them and into the house. He had to find the money. That was his next job.

It was two nights later, and Longarm was sitting in a hotel room trying to finish his report. In the morning he was going to take a train that would get him into

Phoenix. There he was going to turn over to Arizona authorities the money he had recovered, along with a copy of his report that would give an account of what had happened since the robbery. He had written it pretty much as it had happened, including his deal with Jack Shaw to take the outlaw to New Mexico Territory. The Arizona authorities could make of that what they wanted. It was how it had happened and the way Longarm had seen to play it for the best. If they wanted to judge him, that was their business. He was damned if he would lie for anyone.

Except he couldn't finish the report. He had written everything up to where Shaw had come out of the shed. He had written, "Culprit had taken refuge in a small shed, refusing to surrender. Federal officer had warned culprit shots would be fired through the thin walls of shed. Culprit had thrown open door and charged officer. Culprit . . ."

He had stopped at that point. He didn't want to write that Shaw had charged him with a little burnt stick in his hand, forcing Longarm to shoot him in that instant of uncertainty. Jack Shaw was a lot of things, had been a lot of things, but he hadn't been a coward. He just couldn't stand the idea of being pent up and killed by people he didn't know. He'd asked Longarm to do the job. And maybe, even though he'd denied it, there had been some repentance about what he'd done with his life, about some of the meanness he'd shown. Hell, there was no use telling all of Jack's secrets. He couldn't do any more harm. Might as well let him get away with his last little trick.

Longarm inked his pen and then wrote, "Culprit charged federal officer, forcing officer to defend himself. Culprit Jack Shaw was killed by a single bullet to the chest. He had no last words."

Longarm put down the pen and took up his glass of whiskey. He had a drink, and then looked out the window at the dark. Jack might have made a friend if he hadn't gotten confused, Longarm thought. But he at least deserved to go out the way he wanted to. Long-arm yawned. He was tired and weary. He would be ready to get back to Denver and take it easy for a while. Seemed like the rough life got harder every year. He shook his head and finished his whiskey. He was going to sleep that night.

Watch for

LONGARM AND THE DAUGHTERS OF DEATH

205th in the bold LONGARM series
from Jove

Coming in January!

If you enjoyed this book, subscribe now and get...

TWO FREE

A $7.00 VALUE–

If you would like to read more of the very best, most exciting, adventurous, action-packed Westerns being published today, you'll want to subscribe to True Value's Western Home Subscription Service.

Each month the editors of True Value will select the 6 very best Westerns from America's leading publishers for special readers like you. You'll be able to preview these new titles as soon as they are published, *FREE* for ten days with no obligation!

TWO FREE BOOKS

When you subscribe, we'll send you your first month's shipment of the newest and best 6 Westerns for you to preview. With your first shipment, two of these books will be yours as our introductory gift to you absolutely *FREE* (a $7.00 value), regardless of what you decide to do. If you like them, as much as we think you will, keep all six books but pay for just 4 at the low subscriber rate of just $2.75 each. If you decide to return them, keep 2 of the titles as our gift. No obligation.

Special Subscriber Savings

When you become a True Value subscriber you'll save money several ways. First, all regular monthly selections will be billed at the low subscriber price of just $2.75 each. That's at least a savings of $4.50 each month below the publishers price. Second, there is never any shipping, handling or other hidden charges—*Free home delivery*. What's more there is no minimum number of books you must buy, you may return any selection for full credit and you can cancel your subscription at any time. A TRUE VALUE!

LONGARM

Explore the exciting Old West with one of the men who made it wild!